Hotlanta

Also by Denene Millner and Mitzi Miller
(with Angela Burt-Murray)

The Angry Black Woman's Guide to Life

The Vow

Also by Denene Millner

The Sistahs' Rules:
Secrets for Meeting, Getting, and
Keeping a Good Black Man

Dreamgirls

Also by Denene Millner
(with Nick Chiles)

What Brothers Think, What Sistahs Know

What Brothers Think, What Sistahs Know about Sex:
The Real Deal on Passion, Loving, and Intimacy

Money, Power, Respect:
What Brothers Think, What Sistahs Know

Love Don't Live Here Anymore

In Love & War

A Love Story

HOTLANTA

DENENE MILLNER
MITZI MILLER

Point

All rights reserved. Published by POINT, an imprint of Scholastic Inc., *Publishers since 1920*. SCHOLASTIC, POINT, and associated logos are trademarks and/or registered trademarks of Scholastic Inc.

Library of Congress Cataloging-in-Publication Data

Millner, Denene.
    Hotlanta / Denene Millner [and] Mitzi Miller. — 1st ed.
        p. cm. — (Hotlanta)
    Summary: Living a privileged life in Atlanta, wealthy and beautiful African American twin sisters, Sydney and Lauren, must deal with family secrets and scandal when their father is released from prison.
    ISBN-13: 978-0-545-00308-7 (alk. paper)
    ISBN-10: 0-545-00308-3 (alk. paper)
    [1. Sisters — Fiction. 2. Twins — Fiction. 3. Wealth — Fiction.
4. Fathers and daughters — Fiction. 5. African Americans — Fiction.
6. Atlanta (Ga.) — Fiction.] I. Miller, Mitzi. II. Title.
    PZ7.M63957Ho 2008
    [Fic] — dc22

                                                            2007027283

12 11 10 9 8 7 6 5 4 3   10 11 12 13/0

Printed in the U.S.A.
First edition, April 2008

Book design by Steve Scott. Text set in Bulmer, Peignot, and Delta Jaeger.

For Family . . . with arms that hold you tight, there is no need to fear the dark place. There's no place like home.

HOTLANTA

1

SYDNEY

"Sydney! Sydney Duke! I need you downstairs, right now!"

The shrill sound of Sydney's mother's voice echoed all the way up her polished mahogany staircase, down the plush off-white carpeted hall, and right through the walls of Sydney's bedroom.

"I'm coming!" Sydney shouted back as she reluctantly earmarked the page she was reading in the latest issue of *Teen Vogue* and turned off the flat screen where the final minutes of her *Girlfriends* rerun was showing for the millionth time. She snatched up her hot-pink Marc Jacobs bag and matching jean jacket, even though Atlanta and the surrounding suburbs were still warm in late September. Nothing irked her more than when her mother yelled through the house like a wild banshee, but from the tone of her mother's voice, Sydney knew she needed to hurry downstairs and deal with whatever drama awaited before her ride arrived.

She had barely entered the kitchen before her mother started in on her. "Sweetie, I really think this time I may have found the perfect dress for you!"

"Honestly, Mom. The way you were screaming, I thought this was a life-threatening emergency." Sydney grabbed a handful of grapes from the crystal fruit bowl.

"This *is* an emergency. We only have a few weeks left, and Lord knows it'll take at least that long to find both you and your sister the perfect dresses."

"I suppose," Sydney sighed, leaning over her mother's shoulder to glance at the dog-eared page of the October issue of *Vanity Fair* that lay open. "Um, as much as I love Roberto Cavalli's dresses for — I don't know — the MTV Awards, don't you think it's a bit flashy for your party?" she hinted none too subtly, after quickly perusing the over-the-top, beaded, strapless creation shown in the fashion layout. "How about a dress with a little understated elegance? Something more along the lines of Tracy Reese."

Her mother rolled her eyes. "Nothing about my twelve-year-anniversary party is going to be described as understated. And there's no way I, Keisha Duke, will allow either of my daughters to blend in with the crowd on such a big and very expensive night in honor of our family. So you can just forget about Tracy Reese."

"Mom," Sydney pleaded. "She's one of my favorite designers!"

"And that's fine, but the answer is still no. You can wave your little power-to-the-people fist and support black designers all you want when it's your event, but there's no way I'm going to let my friends think we suffer from everyday-people taste. Period." Keisha Duke rarely bothered to hide her need to keep way ahead of the Joneses. She flipped to another page and ran a finger over a picture showing a slinky black number with raw seams and a plunging neckline. "Well, what about Stella McCartney? She's couture and vegan."

Three quick beeps from Carmen's car horn sounded through the open bay windows. "I'll tell you what: Why don't you keep doing your research while I'm at my committee meeting?" Sydney broke for the front door. "Don't forget, I have a movie date with Marcus afterwards, so I might be home a little late."

"Marcus, Usher, Ne-Yo, or whomever you think you're in love with this week, I expect you home no later than one A.M., young lady. And tell Carmen this better be the last time she beeps any car horn in front of my house. This ain't the projects!"

"Yes, Mother," Sydney tossed over her shoulder, rushing toward freedom. She was more aware of that than anyone.

Despite the fact that it was almost seven o'clock, the sky was still fairly bright, and a soft Georgia breeze greeted Sydney as she stepped out the massive front door and ran down the marble steps of the Duke estate.

The sharp smell of newly cut grass burned inside her nose, as she waved hello to the workers dotting the front grounds. Like clockwork, they arrived every Friday afternoon to mow the lawn, trim the hedges, and tend to the exotic flowers that decorated the impressive three-acre property. Keisha Duke might have been a certified control freak when it came to keeping up appearances, but at the end of the day, everything she touched looked amazing. Their home was easily one of the most admired in the exclusive, multimillion-dollar Buckhead subdivision, if not in all of the surrounding Atlanta area.

"What's up, Syd?" Carmen asked as Sydney settled herself in her best friend's car. Since the day when they'd been lined up in height order and Carmen had been placed directly behind Sydney at their exclusive Montessori kindergarten orientation class, Carmen had been extremely comfortable being Sydney's faithful follower. The only place where Carmen didn't trace Sydney's footsteps was in all her charity work, which cut down a great deal of their one-on-one face time.

"Just happy to see the end of another busy week. Your timing is on point, as usual," Sydney said, fiddling with the XM radio.

Carmen pulled her birthday present — a black Land Rover Freelander — around the fountain and back down the Dukes' lengthy driveway.

"You think? It's almost seven. We're barely going to make the start of the meeting. I got caught up looking at the latest update on YoungRichandTriflin.com."

"Umm, I just don't know why you waste so much time reading YRT. You know that it's written by some hater who you probably don't even speak to and has nothing better to do than talk about people and their personal business," Sydney answered with a roll of her eyes. Recently, everyone in school had become obsessed with the scandalous blog started by an anonymous Brookhaven student. Every week all the latest news, trends, and hot gossip from the Atlanta region's most exclusive private high schools was broadcasted to everyone that logged on. Occasionally, if the gossip proved juicy enough, the site administrator would send out a special all-alert bulletin. Not that Sydney would ever admit it, but she too was totally addicted.

"I bet you'll be glad I waste so much time on it if something gets posted about you or your man one of these days. . . ."

"Yeah, yeah, yeah. Regardless, I'm not talking about that, Carmen. I'm talking about saving me from my mother's latest party-dress intervention. She's treating her anniversary soiree like it's Atlanta's answer to the Grammy Awards. If I don't settle on a dress soon, she'll have me wearing some god-awful, neon-pink Versace monstrosity, talking about how she saw Vivica Fox wearing one in *US Weekly*. And forget about Marcus — you already know he's pickier than Keisha if the two of us are going to an event together."

"You don't say," murmured Carmen sarcastically. As much as she liked Marcus, Carmen was one of the few people who had no qualms saying something when his control-freak tendencies got crazy.

"Whatever, Carm . . ." Sydney laughed as she pulled down the visor to check her hair. Lord knew it only took a minute for it to go from curly to frizzy. Since tonight would be her first real alone time with Marcus since the hectic school year had begun, she wanted to make the most of it. And she hoped her hair would cooperate.

Twenty minutes later, they pulled up to the student parking lot at Brookhaven Preparatory School. The enormous state-of-the-art institution was located on a ten-acre plot of land formerly purchased by a Baptist church in the late 1800s for the sole purpose of educating the upper-class Confederate children in the ways of the Bible. Some hundred years later — 1980 to be exact — the property landed in the hands of an anonymous African-American millionaire who promptly turned the rundown estate into the premier, predominantly African-American private institution of learning in the Atlanta area. Catering to the sons and daughters of Atlanta's most well-to-do, Brookhaven boasted a ten-to-one student-to-teacher ratio, laptops and wireless access for all students, a solar-paneled greenhouse, auditoriums with international video-conference capabilities, and a competitive athletics program that included everything from football to polo. And thanks to all the generous donations from alumni and the wealthy families clamoring to gain acceptance for their children, it managed to remain extremely selective (read: African-American applicants always received preferential treatment) and ranked as one of the highest among all secondary schools in Georgia.

At 7:00 P.M. on a Friday, there were only a few cars scattered around the large lot. Sydney recognized the ones that belonged to the other members of the annual Homecoming Benefit Gala planning committee, because they were all chromed-out and shiny. She assumed that the more beat-up rides belonged to either the janitorial staff or the scholarship kids.

"You ready, my dear?" Carmen asked, opening her car door. Wearing a mint-green cashmere cardigan over a white tank top and a cute pair of gray Joe's, Carmen looked every bit the only child of an older, extremely wealthy set of parents.

"Absolutely," Sydney said, shuffling some papers together. "I just reviewed the budget, and it looks like we're in great shape. This should go down no problem."

Carmen clicked the car alarm and headed toward the entrance. "That's what I like to hear. These meetings have been all about the drama, and I just don't have the time for that tonight. I'm trying to get out of here and start the weekend off with something fun."

"You and me both," Sydney agreed. The girls started walking up the stairs toward the entrance.

Almost an hour later, Sydney was beyond pissed. Not because the meeting was particularly difficult. Sure, there'd been a few objections to the chosen tablecloth color and a heated debate over the contents of the gift bags, but Sydney had pacified all parties with the smoothness of Atlanta's mayor, Shirley Franklin. Still, she was aggravated because her Tag read quarter to eight, and not one of the six text messages she'd sent Marcus in the past thirty minutes had been returned. With each one she hammered out, Sydney lost focus on her surroundings.

"So do you agree or not, Sydney? 'Cause we really need to make a decision on this tonight. This issue is, like, a cornerstone of the benefit. And I certainly don't want to jeopardize our fund-raising abilities by dropping the ball." Dawn's insistent voice interrupted her thoughts. Sydney looked up from her iPhone to find the entire Benefit Gala planning committee staring her down.

Damn. There were a lot of perks to being committee chair: It looked great on college apps, Marcus loved it when she took leadership roles in her volunteer efforts, and Sydney not so secretly enjoyed running the show. But right now, she didn't really care about any of that.

"You guys should just take a quick vote instead of relying on my opinion."

"Good idea," said Carmen, rallying to her defense. "I mean, they're just napkin holders, Dawn."

"Excuse me. I need to go to the bathroom," Sydney said, rising out of her seat at the head of the conference room table, leaving Dawn behind with a puckered scowl.

Sydney knew that Dawn had noticed her sending off that last text and had tried to play her in front of everyone on purpose. What a hater. Dawn had been giving Sydney major attitude ever since her not-so-special-looking boyfriend, Alonzo, had dumped her the minute Sydney's twin sister, Lauren, expressed a mild interest in his not-so-special-looking self. Sydney could've saved him the trouble. The last thing on Lauren's mind was a long-term relationship. She fell in and out of love more often than most people with full-time maids changed their monogrammed hand towels. The only reason Lonzo had even registered on her meter was that he was rumored to be the next varsity basketball captain. The poor loser had barely saved Lauren's cell number in his

Sidekick before it was announced that he wasn't picked and Lauren was on to her next flavor of the month.

Quite honestly, Sydney was tired of dealing with the overflow of Lauren drama. Sydney was not Lauren. Why couldn't people get that through their thick skulls?

Lauren specialized in being a superficial, self-centered, scandalous drama queen. All Sydney wanted was to graduate at the top of her class, attend the university of her choice (Brown), marry the man of her dreams (Marcus), and join the exclusive ranks of the country's Who's Who on the society pages of *Vanity Fair* and *Vogue*. Was that really too much to ask?

As soon as she entered the plush lounge area outside of the girls' bathroom, Sydney plopped down on a paisley chaise lounge and whipped out her cell phone. She dialed Marcus's number. It went straight to voice mail.

"Hey, Marcus, it's Sydney. Again." She tried to keep her voice light, but it was almost impossible to hide her annoyance. "What are you doing? We have movie plans, right? My meeting is about to be over. Call. Me. Back." She absentmindedly twisted the diamond stud in her right earlobe.

The silence of her iPhone not ringing echoed around her. Marcus was a lot of things but none of them forgetful. He damn well knew that the two of them had plans to go to the movies tonight. There was no reason for him not to answer his cell or return her texts. Ain't no study group session that serious. Feeling anxious, Sydney headed inside to the nearest sink. She waved her hand under the automatic cold water faucet and started washing her already clean hands in an attempt to calm down.

Duke Family rule number one: Never let 'em see you sweat.

As far as their classmates and even their closest friends were concerned, Sydney and Lauren Duke lived fairy tale lives: Their mom had married an old friend and wealthy car dealership owner, Altimus Duke, when the twins were only five. He'd promptly rescued them from their 250-square-foot cinder-block government-housing cell and moved the family into the posh Duke estate, where every single bathroom had its own Jacuzzi tub and heated towel rack. And though she cared deeply about the plight of the less fortunate, at the end of the day, Sydney was very accustomed to life in the lap of luxury. And to getting exactly what she wanted, when she wanted it.

Continuing to rinse her hands, Sydney turned her attention to the reflection in the mirror. With a frustrated sigh she patted down the wiry curls that had popped out of place in the past forty-five minutes. More than anything, Sydney wished her curl pattern were just a little looser so it would have that sexy, boho-chic look that Tracee Ellis Ross rocked on *Girlfriends*. Granted, Sydney loved her curls, but sometimes she just wished Marcus would step down off his all-natural-beauty soapbox long enough for her mom's hair-dresser to put the occasional quick press in it.

Though Lord knew, Sydney would never utter another bad word about her 'fro if her rather significant bottom would disappear. Sure, most black folks considered the tiny waist and huge booty combo that the identical twins shared off the chain, but not Sydney. She'd have given anything to drop about ten pounds and be a perfect size four. Not too big, not too small: just right. If Lauren thought it was cute to look all soft and squishy, that was her business. Sydney was focused on losing some of the junk in her trunk before the Benefit Gala, even if she had to live on nothing but diet pills, wheat grass, and vitamin water to do it.

Several deep breaths later, Sydney's heart rate finally decreased enough for her to remove her hands from under the faucet. As she turned toward the hand towel dispenser, the sudden vibration in her back pocket startled her. Forgetting all about her dripping hands, Sydney quickly pulled the cell out and answered the call. "This is Sydney," she eagerly offered.

"Hey there, Ladybug," a deep, raspy voice responded.

Sydney faltered momentarily. "Dice? I mean . . . Daddy?" she stuttered in shock.

"Yes ma'am. It's me," the distinctive voice continued as Sydney's heart rate started to race again. "I'm home, sweetie. Your daddy is finally home."

Contrary to the static-filled, faraway-sounding collect calls from the Georgia State Correctional Facility that Sydney had become accustomed to over the past eleven years, Dice Jackson — the twins' biological father — sounded impressively clear . . . and near. "What? When? How?" she questioned as the water dripped down her arms and onto her jacket.

"They released me early this afternoon," he continued.

"But you didn't tell me . . . I mean, where are you now?" Sydney responded, still trying to get her bearings. The moment Sydney had anticipated for over half her life had finally arrived. Somehow, she'd never envisioned it happening while she was hiding out inside the Brookhaven bathroom.

"I know, I know. I didn't want to say anything, get your hopes up, and then have to disappoint my angel again. But I'm here now. I'm at your Aunt Lorraine's and I want to see you . . . and your sister."

2
LAUREN

"Oh, damn!" Lauren yelled as she tossed her MAC Lipglass onto the passenger seat and swerved on two wheels onto Brockett Road, narrowly missing the rear bumper of a broken-down car parked at the intersection. The light from a busted street lamp glinted through her windshield, the glare making it almost impossible to see. Stars dotted the dark sky and the night air was crisp; traces of the evening's flash thunderstorm made shallow puddles inside the street's potholes.

She breathed a sigh of relief that this time she'd recovered without crashing. In the two years since she'd gotten her learner's permit, she'd had enough accidents to almost double her stepfather's car insurance rates and give him enough reasons to bar her from Baby, her shiny black Saab convertible, forever. And driving privileges were a must if she was going to make it to all the go-sees Darryl, her new modeling/ talent agent, was lining up for her each weekend. She sure as hell couldn't count on her sister to take her — she was too preoccupied with saving the world, planning the Homecoming Benefit Gala, and being all up in her trifling boyfriend Marcus's face to actually give a crap about helping Lauren out.

"Cash rules everything around me, Cream! Get the money, dolla dolla bills y'all!" Lauren bobbed her head along with the Wu-Tang Clan CD she was playing for inspiration as she pulled into the decrepit parking lot strewn with empty beer bottles and other assorted litter. This was where Trip Johnson, the famous rap video director, would decide which girls got to star in the video for Thug Heaven's next single. Lauren was convinced this was where she was going to become famous.

The blast of music from Lauren's cell phone interrupted her impromptu Wu-Tang karaoke moment. "You all right?" Lauren heard her kinda-sorta boyfriend, Donald Aller, yelling into her phone. "What's all that screaming? And why you sound all out of breath?"

"I was rapping, loser." Lauren laughed. "I thought I wasn't ever going to get here — damn Friday evening traffic."

"So, nobody in your family knows where you are right now?" Donald questioned.

"Are you kidding me? Keisha Duke would rather lay

down in the driveway and let me climb behind the wheel of the family CL5 and drive full speed over her prone body, then back up and do it again and again before she'd approve of her precious seventeen-year-old daughter traveling to the hood to stuff her ass into an extra-small pair of La Perla hot pants and shake her half-naked badonkadonk in the new Thug Heaven video. In the Swats, no less." Lauren laughed. "Ain't no way. They think I'm at practice.

"My agent told me I have a serious shot at this one," Lauren said to Donald as she turned off the engine and checked her hair in the rearview mirror. "He said all I have to do is show up in something hot and super sexy and be ready to impress Trip with my moves."

"You been practicing, right?"

"Come on now — I've been studying BET like it's the SAT. You don't have to be a rocket scientist to know what they're looking for: You gotta be pretty, have long hair, know how to dance, and be real limber. Oh, and show more skin than clothes."

"Well, ain't no doubt you fit all those categories." Donald laughed.

"Damn, Skippy. I'm about to pimp this right here," she said as she took a swig of Diet Coke, dusted bronzer on her face, and fished around for her misplaced Lipglass — the latest shade of the Viva Glam collection was her current obsession. "Okay, gotta run," she told Donald.

"All right, sweetie — break a leg."

"Call you later," she said, and hung up the phone. Then she adjusted her cropped blazer and stepped out of the car. Glass crunched under her feet. "We ain't in Buckhead anymore, Dorothy." She laughed to herself as she made her way toward the cameras, consciously putting a little extra twist to her hips for anyone watching. She spotted Dough Boy and Candy Man in the middle of a sea of guys in baggy pants and oversize white T's and jerseys, Heinekens and Red Stripes sweating in their palms. She tossed her hair and put on her best sexy smile.

"Over there," a big, burly, bald-headed bruiser shouted gruffly, folding his arms for emphasis. He was as tall and wide as a wall; Lauren could barely see the crowd beyond his girth.

"Pardon me?" She looked over each of her shoulders to see if he was talking to someone else.

"Pardon you, huh? Let me rephrase." He talked loud enough to draw the attention of a few of Thug Heaven's boys. "Take yo' ass over there with all the other yams and wait your turn. Mr. Pinner will start calling groups out shortly. Thank you."

Dayum!

Embarrassed, Lauren hurried in the direction of his pointed finger. The laughter from the boys filled the air like it was her personal walking soundtrack. Now was all *that* necessary? She was even more jittery when she got to the other side of the parking lot and realized that there were a good forty girls ahead of her — all in various states of undress, looking much more scandalous than even Lauren could muster. They were waiting their turn to dance in groups of three for the choreographer, a random white guy with a pinched-up face, and a white woman who appeared to be as stiff as the clipboard she was holding.

"Next!" the clipboard woman yelled. "Ladies — pay attention! We do not have all night. When it's your turn, do the dance the choreographer demonstrates for you, then step over here to Mr. Pinner, who will let you know if you're in or not. And turn off the damn cell phones!"

Lauren pulled her jacket a little tighter around her chest, then thought better of it when she took another look at the amply exposed skin of the girls in front of her. *Now's not the time to be shy*, she thought as she unfastened the top button, sucked in her stomach, squared her shoulders to make her chest look bigger, and tried to reclaim the warm and fuzzy feeling of confidence she'd had on the drive over.

A couple of the thugs walked over, clapping and rubbing their hands together like they were about to say grace. "There's some hoes in this house, there's some hoes in this house!" one said, breaking out into song. Another walked right up to the two girls standing in front of Lauren and started kicking game.

"So, how bad you wanna be in this video?" one with a twinkling gold grill asked, his eyes moving down from their breasts to their hips. " 'Cause me and Dough, we can make it happen. If you can make it happen," he added. But this time he looked at Lauren.

"Oh, yeah?" one of the girls said, stepping up to him and turning his face back toward hers. "I like a brother who can make it happen, especially if he's bringing Dough."

"That's what I'm talking about," the other guy said, clapping his hands.

"What about you, shawty?" Gold Grill asked in a thick southern drawl, shifting his attention again to Lauren.

Lauren froze. Was he serious? She didn't know whether to puke or run but figured if she didn't say anything he'd leave her alone.

When he realized she wasn't paying him any mind, he got ugly. "Forget you, then. This ain't no place for children. Got plenty 'nuff grown-up ass to go around," he said. The other girls rolled their eyes and fell out laughing.

Just as the group ahead of her reached the clipboard lady, Lauren's Sidekick rang out Cee-Lo's "Closet Freak." It was Sydney.

"What?" she whispered, so that nobody would notice her talking.

"Listen, Daddy called me. He's out. He's staying at Aunt Lorraine's in the West End and he wants us to come see him.

I'm heading over there tomorrow morning before my charity work. You in?"

Lauren reeled back from the phone like it was a scorching eight hundred degrees.

"Lauren? Can you hear me? Where are you? What's with that loud crunk shit?"

"Never mind the music," Lauren snapped as she watched the girls finish the dance and walk over to Mr. Pinner. Just that second, she was sorry that, in a weaker state, in the rush of excitement about securing an agent and her first video go-see, she'd told her twin about the whole video thing. Somewhere, somehow, that mess was going to come back to haunt her — this much, she knew. "I'm busy."

"Did you even hear what I said? Daddy's out. And he wants to see his girls."

"Oh, *now* he wants to see us? Eleven years later?" Lauren snarked. The mere mention of her father dragged up memories of all the family dirt she tried so desperately to forget. Her mom didn't want anything to do with Dice and had forbidden her daughters to contact him under any circumstances. After all Keisha had done to make a better life for them, the idea that Sydney actually kept in touch with the bastard who'd left their family high and dry made her nauseous.

"Whatever," Sydney said, and the phone went dead.

"Damn!" Lauren said between clenched teeth as she looked at her cell to see if that heiffa really had hung up on her. She was about to call her sister back and give her a good and righteous curse-out when Clipboard Lady yelled, "Next!" in her direction.

Lauren put her Sidekick on vibrate, tossed it into her purse, and strutted her way toward the dance area. All distractions aside, she had every intention of nailing her steps, particularly since most of the girls before her hadn't been able to get the choreography. As the captain of the varsity dance team at Brookhaven Prep, she had the uncanny ability to imitate, upon one showing, any choreography presented to her. Not to mention, she knew how to work her sexiness to make the football players' tongues wag.

The music was cued up and the choreographer quickly ran through a tight sequence of steps. She watched him intently and committed them to memory. The music was cued up again, and they were counted down. Five, six, seven, eight!

She and the two girls who were in front of her bounced and threw their hands in the air. Pivot. Pivot. Turn. The music burned through Lauren, and she popped her limbs to the beat. Then she turned to twist into a roll. But instead of going left as directed, Lauren dived right. Right into another girl's breasts.

"Damn!" she yelled, practically falling backward.

"Stop the music — just stop it," Clipboard Lady yelled. "Next!"

"But we didn't even get to finish our routine," one of the girls whined. "She ruined our chance!"

Lauren said nothing. She was shaking. When it came to dancing, she never, ever made mistakes.

"Jessica, send those two over to me," yelled Mr. Pinner, who was standing a few yards away with the entourage, all of whom were grinning from ear to ear.

"What about this one?" Clipboard asked, holding Lauren by the shoulder.

Pinner flicked his wrist away dismissively and turned back to his crew, who by then had circled around the two girls like vultures swooping down on their prey.

Lauren slunk back to her ride.

"Well, if it isn't Pardon Me," someone called out after her. She tried not to give him too much attention — just kept walking. "I'm sayin' if you wanna be down, you could always just *go* down, shawty." He laughed evilly.

Lauren convinced herself not to Marion Jones it the rest of the way to the car, but she locked the doors as soon as she slammed the driver's side shut. Just then, she felt her cell phone vibrating in the purse on her lap. The number was unfamiliar.

"What?" she practically yelled into her phone.

"Hey, baby girl," the man on the other end said slowly. "That the way you always answer your phone?"

Lauren should have expected that her dumb-ass sister would give their sperm donor her cell phone number.

"You got the wrong number," she barked, determined to keep the conversation short and simple.

"Come on, Dewdrop. Don't do me like that," Dice implored, pulling out Lauren's childhood nickname for old time's sake. "Your sister gave me your number. But don't worry, she already warned me that you probably don't want to be bothered with me."

"Well, for once, my sister got the message right," Lauren snapped.

"You need to know I've been wanting to see you for the longest time, but since your mama wouldn't bring y'all to see me . . ." Dice continued.

"First of all, don't blame my mother for us not seeing you. You're the one who got locked up," Lauren said through clenched teeth, cutting her father's sentence short. "Seems like she managed to make all the right decisions for us without you, so don't you ever question her. And second, I ain't Sydney. You may have fooled her into thinking you care, but you're not fooling me. Now if you'll excuse me, I have somewhere to be, and it ain't with you."

"Well, baby girl," Dice said, resignation creeping into his voice, "if you change your mind, I'm at 1315 Hope Street. Your Aunt Lorraine will be happy to let you in."

3
SYDNEY

"Whew. I thought that damn meeting was never going to end," Carmen complained bitterly fifteen minutes later as they finally headed toward the school's exit.

"Who are you telling? I was about to straight fall asleep up in there tonight," chimed in Sydney's other tight girl, Rhea. Sydney and Rhea had become close when they shared the same eighth-grade gym class. Rhea was the daughter of a lawyer and spoke three different languages, her favorite of all being the Angry Black Woman Curse Out. "And for the record, if Dawn said just one more word about the damn napkin holders, I swear I was going to leap across the table and strangle her!"

"You know she could care less about the Gala," Carmen

sneered. "She's just miserable because of what happened with Alonzo."

"Let's change the subject, shall we?" Even though she privately agreed with her girls, as a rule Sydney Duke did not gossip, talk trash, or engage in catty behavior in public. She was better than that. "As long as the Gala is a success, I could care less about Dawn and Alonzo."

"I'm just saying, Syd," Carmen started again, "she needs to stop showing out 'cause she's bitter. Everyone can't be the black Barbie and Ken like you and Marcus."

" 'Marcus and I are going to the movies. Marcus and I are going to feed the homeless. Marcus and I are going to get married.' Marcus, Marcus, Marcus," Rhea mocked Sydney in a high-pitched voice. "I'm surprised you two haven't totally morphed into one person."

"I don't know what you're talking about." Syd hedged as she fingered the new Chanel charm bracelet that Marcus had given her on their fourth anniversary. She tried to casually look toward the school entrance for his car's headlights as she braced for the inevitable "we love Marcus but he takes up all your free time" discussion.

"Sure you don't. And I guess you also haven't noticed that every time we try to make plans with you, it requires two weeks' advance notice because you're constantly overbooked saving the world or spending quality time," Rhea said.

25

"You guys have been complaining about this for as long as Marcus and I have been dating. Don't you ever get tired of repeating yourselves?" Sydney snapped back as they reached the curb. Normally, she would simply pacify her girls with an apology and the promise of a ladies' night out. But little did they know that she literally had to threaten Marcus with bodily harm to even get this little movie date scheduled. So she certainly wasn't about to let them jump all over her because of it.

"Come on now, Sydney," Carmen said, softening. "We're just saying Marcus can't be your whole life."

"My whole life isn't about Marcus!" Sydney insisted as she peeled off her jean jacket. Even though the sun had set, the humidity was getting worse by the second.

"Then prove it," challenged Rhea. "Come with us to check out the AKA's open mic night at the AU Student Union tonight."

Sydney avoided eye contact by fumbling in her purse. "I can't," she sighed. "Marcus will never let me hear the end of it if I skip out on tonight —"

"See?" Rhea taunted, with her hands on her hips. "You say being a strong black woman is a priority, but you're really all about your man."

"Oh, please, Rhea. One thing has nothing to do with the other. Just because I'm happy in my relationship does not mean I'm not a strong black woman or a good friend!"

"You know what? You may be right, Sydney," Rhea spit back. "However, it does mean you're an unavailable friend."

Sydney's mouth dropped open. She instinctively looked to Carmen, who was studiously reapplying her lip gloss, for some backup.

"She's right, Syd," Carmen finally agreed. "I feel like the three of us have barely hung out the last few months, except when we drive to committee meetings and stuff. Marcus is my boy, but the whole drop everything when he calls is so caveman."

"Exactly. Let's go, Carm." Rhea turned on the heel of her boot and stomped off.

"But I'll definitely hit you up later and let you know what you missed, Syd," Carmen called over her shoulder as she followed immediately behind Rhea.

"Whatever." Sydney tapped the redial button on her cell. She wasn't about to defend the time she spent with her man to anybody. Speaking of which, where was Marcus?

Thirty minutes, fifteen text messages, and ten phone calls later, Sydney's ass was still sitting on the curb, and she was fuming. A mere two months ago, something like this would never have happened.

Seriously.

Until two months ago, Marcus was the perfect boyfriend. Cosigned by both Sydney's social-climbing mother and her extremely overprotective stepfather, Marcus Green had a reputation for outstanding community service and stellar academic achievement that had been well established since the seventh grade. It seemed only natural that he, the official good-black-man in training, and Sydney, the Duke family's golden girl, would be together. Not to mention how much Marcus's mother, Ms. Althena Green (the hard-nosed, revolutionary, former Black Panther–turned–city councilwoman), L-O-V-E-D Sydney. Both parents and peers admired the couple equally. Aside from his occasionally controlling, slightly chauvinistic, somewhat opportunistic attitude, Marcus Green was the cream of Atlanta's young, progressive African-American crop. And simply put, life couldn't have gotten any better — except that for some reason, ever since junior year had started two months ago, Marcus had been acting real funny.

Sydney knew Marcus was busy studying for the SAT on top of his numerous extracurricular activities. But dammit, she was, too. Yet she found the time in her busy schedule to try to make room for their relationship. Whenever she tried to talk to him about it or about the distance growing between them, he insisted she was being emotional and overreacting. But now he had her sitting out in front of a deserted high school in the middle of the night because he wouldn't answer his phone. And there was nothing emotional about that.

The sudden sound of leaves rustling startled Sydney. What was once a gentle breeze had now picked up into an aggressive wind that threatened to usher in a late-night rain-storm. She instinctively stood up and headed back toward the well-lit area at the top of the stairs. About ten steps up, the sound of footsteps stopped her dead in her tracks. Sydney turned around, expecting to see Marcus.

"What's up, Sydney?"

"Jason Danden, you scared the crap outta me!" she called out against the wind as the school's star football player appeared at the bottom of the stairs. She retreated back down to curb level.

"My bad, ma. I didn't mean to scare you. I was just rush-ing to get home so I can catch up with the rest of the team at South City Kitchen."

The thought of soul food from South City made Sydney's mouth water. "No worries," she said, noticing how much bigger Jason's chest had become over the summer. This boy was no joke. Ever since he and his family had moved down to Atlanta from New York their freshman year, he'd just gotten better and better looking. Not to mention, more and more popular.

"So what are you doing out here so late?"

"Um, what are *you* doing out here, Mr. Lots-of-Questions? If I'm not mistaken, didn't football practice end about thirty minutes ago?"

"Oh, true, I didn't mean to be all up in ya business like that. . . ." Jason shyly stepped back. "You ain't got to tell me nothing."

"Oh, I was just playing with you, Jason," Sydney said. "I was actually waiting for my . . . sister. Lauren is supposed to be picking me up, and no big surprise, she's running late."

"Oh, okay. Well, I'm still here because Coach wanted to talk to me about some secret play he's formulating for this weekend's game against the Wolverines," Jason answered with a diffident smile. "But don't ask for details, 'cause this co-captain can't tell you anything."

"Co-captain? Wow! Is a Yankee boy trying to run the A?"

"Aww, not me," Jason continued modestly, "but being named co-captain as a junior is a good look. I'm definitely trying to get that football scholarship when the time comes."

"Not that your family needs the scholarship, but I'm sure you'll make it happen," she said, moving closer to allow his body to block the wind that was picking up. As the storm clouds lurked ominously overhead, Sydney wished she'd thought to wear her new Louis Vuitton rainboots.

"Yeah, I guess . . ."

"Don't guess. You gotta know," she corrected him gently.

"Yo, you're right, Sydney."

"You make me sound like a little know-it-all." She nervously looked around him to make sure they were really alone. Last thing she needed was Marcus showing up and getting the wrong idea.

"Naw, not at all. Beauty and brains is a hot combo."

Whoa. Hold up. Did Jason Danden, future football star and all-around hottie, just call Sydney Duke beautiful? Despite the twins' nearly identical looks, thanks to her long-flowing and extremely expensive weave most guys considered Lauren the beautiful twin. Add to that Sydney's conservative attitude and refusal to follow every new hoochie-mama trend, and, well, let's just say she'd long grown accustomed to Lauren outshining her in the "hotness" department.

"I don't know about all that, but I appreciate you clarifying." Sydney scuffed her new Gucci loafers on the pavement.

"I'm saying, I don't feel right leaving you here by yourself. Can I give you a ride home? Or you could always roll out tonight with me if you like. You know, grab a bite with the team . . ."

"Jason, now you know I got a man! Why you trying to get me in trouble?"

Sydney could certainly appreciate Southern hospitality as much as the next chick, but there was no way she was about to show up at South City Kitchen on a Friday night with Jason Danden. It wouldn't take but two seconds for Marcus to hear about that. Sydney knew he'd answer his damn phone for *that* information.

"Hey, all I'm saying is it's dark, the sky is about two seconds from opening up, and you shouldn't be alone out here."

With streaks of lightning cracking in the distance, the enormous school looked like something straight out of the opening scene from the next blockbuster horror film. Sydney glanced around the now completely deserted parking lot. Public perception be damned, Sydney Duke wasn't spending one more minute alone in the dark. "On second thought, you know what? I would love a ride home. Thank you."

"Bet. My ride is parked over there," he said, nodding toward a dark blue Tahoe SUV as he bent down to pick up her book bag. Like the exterior of the truck, the interior was spit-shined and even smelled of wildberry car freshener. Sydney shifted in her seat to sneak a good look at the immaculate backseat and wondered how it would feel to be stretched out back there. She quickly turned around and caught Jason peeking at her out of the corner of his eye.

"What?" she asked suspiciously, thankful that he couldn't read her mind.

"Nothing. You good?"

"Just fine, thanks." Her gaze fell on his hand gripping the gearshift. His nails were perfectly trimmed. She forced herself to stare out the windshield and concentrate on the road.

Twenty minutes later, Jason parked his car in her driveway and turned the headlights off. They both stared at the illuminated water fountain in front of the bleached-brick-and-stucco mansion. Raindrops pitter-pattered around them.

"It was cool getting to spend some time with you."

"Ditto." Sydney unbuckled her seat belt. "And I really appreciate the lift. Although I must admit, I haven't sat through that much crunk music in my life!"

"All righty, Miss Mainstream. If I promise to only play Mary J and Justin Timberlake, will you call me sometime?"

"I mean, as long as your girlfriend is okay with that," she hinted coyly about Jason's girlfriend, who had graduated from Brookhaven the year before.

"Tyra's at Florida A&M now. She ain't thinking about me no more," he answered.

"Oh, I see. Guess I missed that YRT alert, huh?"

"Apparently. But the real question is, will your boy Marcus mind you calling me?" Jason countered with a raised eyebrow.

"Don't you worry, I make sure my man has no reasons to worry," Sydney replied, surprising even herself at how easily she flirted back.

"Well, in that case . . ."

Sydney tapped his numbers into her phone and let herself out of the truck. If it hadn't been so dark and had he looked really close, Jason might've seen Sydney grinning from ear to ear as she ran for the foyer, ducking under her jean jacket and dodging puddles on the toes of her suede loafers.

Sydney had barely closed the door to her bedroom before it reopened. Surprised at the intrusion, she turned to face the only person in the house who never waited for an invitation to enter — her mother.

"Who was that bringing you home in a big ol' truck?"

"Were you spying on me?" Sydney gasped dramatically, putting her hands on her hips.

"I have a right to know about anything that happens on *my* property." Keisha Duke smirked. "I heard a truck, so I looked at the security video."

"Oh." Sydney looked away, unconsciously tugging on that right earlobe again.

"So, who was driving the truck? I thought you were headed to the movies?"

So did she. "Marcus got caught up in a meeting, so Jason Danden was kind enough to offer me a ride home."

"Hmm, Jason Danden. Isn't he that football player I keep reading about in the paper?" her mother asked as she raised one perfectly waxed eyebrow.

"Perhaps," said Syd as she turned away. More than anything she wished her mom would leave the room so she could get back to thinking about her unbelievable ride home.

Mrs. Duke remained undeterred as she pulled her honey-blonde hair up in a twist. "Well, you know how quickly rumors can get started."

"Mother, please. It was just a ride home. And besides, he's so not my type."

"Your type? You don't even know what a type *is* yet. But I'll say this — I saw the grin on your face when you walked in the door. And you better be careful. I didn't work this hard to get us up outta the ghetto your father left us in for you to backslide over some no 'count alleged football prodigy from New York!"

Just as Mrs. Duke's tirade was on the verge of a full crescendo, she was interrupted by a familiar voice. "Hey, hey, what's all the fussing and fighting about?" Relieved, Sydney turned to find her stepfather's impressive six-foot three-inch frame filling her doorway. With his flawless chocolate skin, brooding eyes, and close-cut Caesar haircut, Altimus Duke was definitely considered one of ATL's finest. Strangers often mistook him for the actor who played Stringer Bell on *The Wire*, and the twins caught more than their share of fellow students ogling Altimus when he attended school functions. "Babe, I can hear you flapping your jaws all the way down the hall. What's up?"

"Nothing, Altimus. Mom is tripping 'cause I caught a ride home with a guy before she had a chance to run a complete background check on him *and* his entire family," Sydney offered with an eye roll.

"Ain't nobody tripping. I'm just making sure that *my*

child doesn't find herself right back where her no-good daddy left us," Keisha corrected with a huff as Altimus sauntered over and enveloped her from behind in a hug.

"Relax, Keish, Syd's a good kid," he said as he nuzzled her neck. "You don't gotta badmouth her father for her not to end up in the hood." He looked over Keisha's shoulder at Sydney knowingly.

"Whatever, she'd better not," Keisha pouted, immediately deferring to Altimus's authoritative tone.

"Uh, yeah, thanks for the vote of confidence. And if the two of you are finished getting all hugged up in my room, I'd like to do some homework before I go to sleep," she responded sarcastically.

"You know I always got your back, princess," Altimus laughed as he ushered Keisha out of the room. "Don't stay up too late, babe."

"And you know, I'm dead-ass serious," Mrs. Duke added over her retreating shoulder for emphasis.

As the two disappeared down the hall, Sydney reclosed the door with a firm snap. Nothing annoyed her more than when her mother brought up the twins' biological father. Even though — as usual — Altimus had managed to shut her down, Keisha's harsh words still stung. Sure, the convicted gun smuggler was less than Atlanta's most upstanding citizen, but as far as Sydney was concerned, Dice was still a good man. And Sydney worshipped the ground he walked on.

Turning toward the waiting pile of textbooks on her desk, Sydney allowed a smirk to cross her face. She could only imagine what her know-it-all mother would say if she knew Sydney was planning to see the very same biological father she'd just finished bashing . . . first thing in the morning.

4
LAUREN

Lauren could hardly see straight through her tears as she pro-grammed 1315 Hope Street into the navigation system — yet another seedy, shady place where she didn't have any business going. Four wrong turns, two near-accidents, one gas station stop later, and she finally parked across from her destination, still unsure just what the hell possessed her to — or why — she was taking Dice up on his offer to visit. She'd sat in the parking lot of a gas station not too far from the video shoot for a half hour, replaying their short conversation in her mind, alter-nately pissed that he'd called at all and giddy at the fact that her father truly wanted to see her, despite that her mom had insisted to her and her sister all those years their dad was in prison that he didn't want any contact. If that were indeed the case, why would Dice's first call out the pen be to his daughters, Lauren asked herself. But if he really cared, like he was trying to make himself sound over the phone, why didn't he try to keep in contact with them while he was locked up? Could he have kept in touch? *Do they even let inmates have stamps?* she asked herself. At 8:30 P.M., Lauren wanted to confront him — tell him face-to-face that he wasn't shit and that he better stop dialing her number. By 8:32, every inch of her wanted to look into her biological's eyes, feel his embrace — find out for sure why he didn't fight harder to stay out of prison and be with his girls. When the neon orange 8:34 lit up her dashboard, Lauren was so paralyzed by indecision that the hot tears wouldn't stop coming. Just fifty yards away was her father, and all she could think about was what he might look like. Would he be a gray, old, haggard, beat-down version of the handsome, strong man she used to love to hang on? Or would he be muscular and packed, like the buff, crazy psychopaths in that HBO show *Oz*?

God. Her father could be one of those guys.

Too nervous to get out of the car, Lauren called her girl, Dara, to calm her nerves.

"What up? Where you at?" she said, trying to sound cheerful.

"We're in the Commons, watching JV stumble through their routines," Dara dragged, her disgust evident.

"Dang, it's Friday night — no weekend hiatus for hazing?" Lauren laughed through her tears.

"I swear, these scrubs will never make it onto varsity with those sorry-ass moves." To the junior varsity girls, she yelled, "Pick up your feet! Pop it! Damn — what are y'all doing, auditioning for *Elmo's World*? This is ridiculous! It's step, step, hop, hop, pop, half turn, kick, pop!"

"Damn, D, is it that bad?" Lauren asked, fishing a tissue out from her glove compartment.

"Do you really want to know?"

"Um, not really. How long you gotta lounge with the lames? Because I could really use a shoulder to lean on right now."

"What happened? You didn't get picked for the lead in the video? Relegated to background dancer?" she asked.

Lauren cursed herself again for having bragged earlier about how she'd be *the* flyest chick strolling the hallways of Brookhaven Prep once everybody saw her getting her Melissa Ford on in the latest video from the A's most famous rapper. But she'd recover. She always did. "Long story," Lauren said. "Anyhow, I got my stepfather's platinum AmEx, and I'm ready to do damage. Wanna meet me at my house? I kinda need to be getting back anyway before my parents realize I wasn't really with Donald."

"True. I'll call my mom and tell her I'm stopping by your place on my way home," Dara said, and hung up.

That right there was why Lauren loved her some Dara, regardless of all the drama that had gone down. Not too long ago, Lauren had caught Dara with Marcus's tongue dangling between her lips during a fund-raiser at the High Museum of Art while Sydney was working the room for donations.

Dara and Marcus had been all booed up in an obscure corner just off the entrance of the second-level bathroom, twisted in a furiously passionate tangle. They'd been going at it so heavy that it took a few beats longer than it should have for them to respond to Lauren's "What the hell are you two doing?"

"Ohmigod! Ohmigod! Ohmigod!" Dara had exclaimed, pushing Marcus off of her and tugging her dress down, broken lengths of beading falling at her feet like hail. Marcus had tried to turn his back to Lauren at first, but, realizing there was nowhere to go, he finally faced her. He'd absentmindedly run his hands over his locks; his eyes were cast downward, no doubt in embarrassment.

Lauren grabbed her BFF by the arm and yanked her off to the bathroom. She could smell Marcus's dreadlock hair cream on Dara as she pushed past her — a scent Lauren despised. Whenever Marcus was at their house for longer than a few minutes, Lauren would have the housekeeper, Edwina, run through all the common areas with the deodorizer to get rid of his stench.

"You're not going to tell Sydney, are you?" Dara had pleaded. "I know how this looks, but you gotta trust me. There's nothing going on between Marcus and me. And if you tell your sister, it's going to turn into a big mess."

Dara was right. Sydney would manage to turn what her dog of a boyfriend did into yet another issue to blame on Lauren. It would be just like her to think that Lauren had had something to do with hooking up her self-righteous, power-to-the-people, fake-ass backpacker boyfriend with precisely the kind of girl he and Sydney railed against: a light-skinned, green-eyed, half-white girl who looked the exact opposite of what Sydney was and what Marcus claimed to love.

"Fine," Lauren had quietly conceded. And then she moved in closer to Dara's face to make her next point. "But that *is* my sister's boyfriend. Whatever was going on between you two ends tonight. I'm not trying to have this come back on my ass, got it?"

Lauren snapped out of her haze and used the back of her hand to wipe her tears when she realized she had company on her aunt's street. A crowd of what could only be described as Men of Unclear Purpose wandered by, looking like they were about to stir up some trouble. Someone whistled and ran his hand along the passenger side. "Yo, peep this ride!"

Lauren, beyond unnerved by the menacing crowd, put her car in gear and tried to make a speedy getaway, but in her haste, she didn't realize Baby was in reverse, and she smashed into the car parked behind her.

"Yo! What the hell are you doing?" one of the boys in the crowd cried, while the others pointed and sent up a chorus of "Oh, snap!" She pushed down the automatic-lock button and said a silent "screw me" for being in front of Aunt Lorraine's busted-up house in the first place.

"My ride's all dented up!" the boy yelled.

Lauren met his eyes in her rearview mirror. He had the flat of his hand raised like a traffic cop. He did not look happy, but he did look cute. His eyes were big and brown with heavy lids, making him look almost Asian. Lips, thick. Teeth, sparkling. High cheekbones. Cropped haircut. Chocolate. Fine. Under normal circumstances, Lauren would have pimped this moment, but Cute Boy's friends made her want to call 911.

"Yo, shorty jacked you up, son," one yelled.

"Must be lost or somethin', stylin' in the fly ride in these parts," another said.

Lauren wasn't getting out of the car for nothing. But then Cutie got a closer look at her and started shooing his friends away. "Let me handle this — I'll catch y'all later."

"You sure you can handle that?" one of the Men of Unclear Purpose questioned.

"Fall back," he said. "I got this, man."

Cute Boy let his friends get far enough away before he turned his full attention to her. "I need to see your driver's license, registration, and your phone so I can call po-po over here to get a report. 'Cause you fixing my ride."

Lauren opened the door and slowly stuck out one leg, then two so he could get the full effect of her shoes and the muscles on her calves and thighs. By the time she stood up, shook out her hair, and smoothed down her jacket, she, not the damaged car, had his full attention.

"Where's your phone?" Lauren asked, shaking her hair for emphasis.

"Relax, sweetie, I left it at home."

"Let's take a look, shall we?" Lauren said sweetly, smiling.

She whipped past him and put enough swing in her hips to make her hair bounce as she made her way to his car. "Damn," she cursed silently. His fender was practically crunched up to the grill of his car, and her back bumper was dented and scratched enough for Altimus to have a small cow over the damage. He'd confiscate Baby for sure, but that was neither here nor there. Lauren needed to figure out a way to defuse the situation at hand so she could get the hell on back to Buckhead. The Altimus situation she would figure out later.

"Oh! It's just a small dent and some readjusting. You can take that to Paintless Dent Removal in downtown Atlanta — they can hook that right on up."

"I think you mean *you* can take it there," he said, softening his tone a little bit.

"I know the guys there — they'll fix it for you and send me the bill."

"Oh, I see, you pushin' the new Saab and got fly con-nects, huh, shorty?"

Ugh. Lauren turned up her nose.

He'd been doing so good until he opened his mouth with all that ruffneck talk. Fine or not, the macho-boy thing wasn't working for her. Lauren walked over to stare up in his face. "My name isn't Shorty. It's Lauren."

"Well, nice to meet you, Lauren," Cute Boy said. "You can tell your hookup that I'll be there tomorrow afternoon, so have your credit card handy. And how exactly do you know a bunch of guys at a body shop? You crash into people often?"

Lauren moved in a little closer to him and said, "Only ones I want to meet."

"Ah-ight. I see Ms. Lauren got game to go with the fancy car and clothes, huh?"

"No game, sweetie — um, what did you say your name was?"

"Jermaine," he said, tossing his chin in her direction and extending his hand. "Jermaine Watson. It's nice to meet you, even under such unfortunate circumstances."

"'Unfortunate' is a bit harsh, don't you think?" Lauren said with a sly smile. "After all, we did meet."

She walked back to her car, reached for her Sidekick, and speed-dialed Hal at Paintless, leaving a message for him to expect Jermaine Watson. "Oh, and um, no need to tell Daddy about this — I'll take care of the charges, same as usual."

Lauren clicked off, tossed her phone back into her car, and curtly explained to Jermaine, "Hal and my dad go back — he does a lot of work for him, so it's no biggie."

"Uh-huh, I see." He laughed. "Definitely not the first time this has happened, huh?" This time, she laughed. Then she looked down at his sneakers. Bright white Air Force Ones. Nice.

"So if I have problems with Hal, how do I get in touch with you?"

"Oh, don't worry, Hal will hook you up, no questions asked."

"Then how does a brother get in touch with you if he wants to see you again?"

"A true gentleman would politely ask for my number."

"Well, I'm a gentleman, and I'd like you to consider this an official request for your number," he said, licking those juicy lips for emphasis.

Lauren didn't say a word. Cute or not, she really didn't know if she wanted a thug calling her phone and trying to come see her. Lauren's mother wouldn't take too kindly to the bottoms of that boy's sagging jeans scraping their front doorstep. And he was crying over a little dent in his raggedy car, like he couldn't afford to pay the couple hundred bucks it would take to pay for the touch-up. No, Lauren quickly decided, Cute Boy couldn't have her number. But she wasn't about to tell him that.

"If you've got skills, you'll find out what my number is and get at me," she said coyly. "In the meantime, I've got to get home. It was nice chatting with you."

"That's it?"

"That's it," she said.

Then Lauren noticed a light go on in the front of Aunt Lorraine's house, which meant that whoever was there — quite possibly Dice — could look out the window at any moment and see her there. And just that moment, she realized that she did not want that. As fun as this flirting was, she needed to get outta there before she was spotted.

"But there is one more thing," she said quickly, with another sly smile, slinking around the backside of her ride.

"What's that, Ms. Lauren?" Jermaine said, punctuating his smug words with an even slicker grin.

"Can you tell me how to get back to Buckhead?"

5
SYDNEY

"I missed you so much, baby girl." Dice Jackson's huge, tattoo-covered arms wrapped themselves around Sydney's small frame.

Sydney relished the feel of her father's protective embrace, though it startled her a bit to feel the grooves of his ribs. His once shiny caramel skin had dulled during his twelve-year stint behind bars, and he looked as tired and raggedy as the old armchair he rose up from. She reminded herself that Dice wasn't back from an extended vacation. On the contrary, he had been released from one of the most notorious prisons in all of Georgia.

"It sure is good to see y'all back together," her Aunt Lorraine chimed in. She was hunched over in a dining room chair she'd dragged to the far corner of the room, wearing a dingy housecoat and run-over slippers. "Lord knows what kinds of trickery you had to use to pick up your dad's letters from here all those times. What with your mama frontin' like she ain't from these same parts. Shoot."

"Mind your business, Lorraine! This girl don't have no control over her mother, so stop talking to her about it," Dice snapped back.

"Well, excuse the hell outta me," she grumbled, turning up the volume on the television and taking a long drag on her Newport.

Unfortunately, her Aunt Lorraine was right. Sydney's mom had gone out of her way to make sure that Lauren and Sydney severed all ties with their father. Whenever either of the twins asked to speak to or visit Dice, Keisha would become furious and threaten them with all kinds of cruel and unusual punishment. She made it very clear that she was not interested in having Dice anywhere near *her* children or *her* new life. Although Altimus normally weighed in on behalf of the girls when Keisha was being over the top, he refused to be involved in the Dice situation. According to him, it was Keisha's right to make the decision.

When Sydney was finally old enough to do some snooping of her own, she found her Aunt Lorraine's address in one of Keisha's old black books. It wasn't long before the headstrong twelve-year-old found a phone number for Aunt Lorraine, who put her in touch with her father. Although twelve years had passed since she'd physically laid eyes on him, thanks to the monthly packet of letters and photos her Aunt Lorraine would sneak to her, Sydney felt as if she knew Dice like the back of her hand.

"Mom can try all she wants, but nothing will keep me away from you again," Sydney said as the two moved over to the torn leather couch.

"I believe you, Ladybug. If only your sister could be as understanding . . ."

Sydney bristled at the mention of Lauren. "Why do you even care what she thinks?" she asked, pulling back from his embrace. After Dice lost his first appeal five years ago, Lauren made it very clear she wanted nothing more to do with her dad.

"'Cause she's my child and I love the both of you equally, Sydney," he whispered. "Deep down, she knows I'm innocent."

"I guess." Sydney pouted, feeling as if any discussion of Lauren unnecessarily detracted from her long-awaited father-daughter quality time.

"Now tell me. What kind of stuff have you been getting into these days?"

Sydney's face lit up. She was happy to steer the subject back to something more positive: herself, naturally. "Well, I'll be glad when this Benefit Gala is finally over. It has been nothing but drama pulling it together. Not for nothing, but if everything goes as planned, my committee will have raised over ten thousand dollars for the new library wing, which is actually a record for any Brookhaven class."

"That's cool, Sydney. Real cool," Dice said as he tucked one of Sydney's flyaway curls behind her ear. "To think that when I got locked up, you were just starting to count your one, two, threes, and now you're raising ten G's and better to help build libraries. Makes me sad that I've missed so much of your life."

"Daddy, we both know that wasn't your fault." She took his callused hand in hers. "I'm just glad you're here now. And I can't wait to make you a part of everything in my life now."

"Yeah. I want to meet this boyfriend of yours. Flex some fatherly muscle in front of this boy. Marcus, wasn't it?" Dice questioned. "You surely wrote a lot about him in all your letters to me."

Sydney's heart dropped. She'd gone to bed last night without hearing from Marcus, only to have him wake her up with a midnight assault of pebbles on her window. He explained he'd had a marathon study session and his cell phone had died. According to his story, as soon as he realized how much time had passed, he'd driven directly over to the Duke mansion to apologize.

But Sydney Duke had pride, almost a bit too much, and refused to go down and speak with him. If Marcus thought some lame excuse and a couple of pathetic-sounding apologies could make up for the humiliation of being left standing in the dark, he should try again. Not that she'd admit it but Carmen and Rhea's stinging accusations of her frequent willingness to revolve her life around Marcus's schedule had struck a chord. Especially now that she saw how nice Jason was toward her. Not that the most upstanding, faithful, devoted girlfriend in Brookhaven Prep would ever think about stepping out on her man. But still.

"He's the smartest, most ambitious guy I know. He's like my soul mate," she said, leaving out the fact that she had yet to tell Marcus her father had been released from prison because she *still* hadn't spoken to him.

"Soul mate, huh? That's a pretty big statement considering how young you are. Just be careful throwing words like *love* and *soul mate* around. Shoot, I can remember a time I used to say the same things about your mother. . . ."

"I guess," Sydney said as she shifted uncomfortably in her seat and looked down at the ratty shag carpet beneath her Chanel ballet flats.

Raising Sydney's face to his, Dice instructed: "Don't guess. Know. Understood?"

"Yes, sir."

"Good. Now you best get out of here, before your mother figures out you're not doing your service work."

"Okay, Dad, but listen. I was thinking, now that you're back here maybe I can talk to Altimus about getting you a job at one of the dealerships. You know, he's so cool, I bet he'd hook it up and never breathe a word about it to Mom if I asked . . ." Sydney leaned into her father's ear and spoke in a low whisper. "I mean, at least it'd give you a way to get out of the house during the day."

"Absolutely not," he said sternly as his face distorted in anger. "I don't want a damn thing from that man."

"Huh?" Sydney reared back in surprise.

"You heard me. This is not open for discussion, Sydney. Just go," he ordered without a blink of his eye.

"Okay, then," she replied meekly as she stood up and headed to the front door. "I guess I'll call you later. Bye, Aunt Lorraine. I love you, Dad," Sydney called out as she walked out.

As she sped down I-20, Sydney found herself consumed with confusion. After all these years, could Dice still be mad because Keisha left him for Altimus? Eventually, the persistent flashing of the message light on Sydney's phone managed to distract her from her thoughts. *Hmm, probably just more messages from Marcus.*

To avoid any sudden impulses to call Marcus and clear the air, Sydney left her phone in the car while she went into the Better Day Women's Shelter. She wanted him to suffer a bit longer. Still, she couldn't stop thinking about him. And even after three hours of cleaning up behind the residents and playing with and feeding lunch to their kids, Marcus was still on her mind.

As she emerged into the late Saturday afternoon, Sydney stopped to consider her options. Normally, she'd call Marcus and see if he was finished tutoring at the local library in Decatur or even hit up the girls for a late lunch at Harry's. But clearly she wasn't on the best terms with any of the three. And while there was that BBQ at Satonja Gilbert's house, there was no way she was rolling solo. She resigned herself to heading back to the house.

There, everything was pretty quiet. Altimus was probably making the rounds of his dealerships, and you could safely bet both girls' college tuition that their mom was at Château Elan getting a deluxe spa treatment. Sometimes it seemed like all Keisha Duke ever did was yell at the girls, plan extravagant parties, go to the spa, and sleep.

Kicking off her shoes, Sydney headed up to her room to relax until it was time for her five-thirty choir rehearsal. Sneaking over to her aunt's house had required waking up earlier than normal to avoid running into Altimus as he returned from his morning jog. Sydney was beat. As she walked by Lauren's room, the sound of laughter from her sister's television attracted her attention. Sydney could see an open laptop sitting precariously close to the edge of the bed, while the top of Lauren's silk scarf–covered head poked out from under the mountain of covers. Unless Lauren had a football game to dance at, she was usually napping and therefore completely antisocial until at least three o'clock in the afternoon on the weekends . . . like mother, like daughter.

When Sydney reached her room, she could tell from the made-up bed and orderly pile of textbooks on her desk that Edwina had already started straightening up on the floor. She had hoped for a little peace and quiet, but her cell's relentless, annoying vibration finally forced her to retrieve it from the bottom of her purse. Scrolling down, she counted eight new messages on her screen.

After listening to all eight of Marcus's pleading messages, Sydney's heart finally melted. Life was too short to be mad. It was almost eighteen hours since she'd last spoken to Marcus. That was a record for the couple that'd been checking in with each other every couple of hours like clockwork for the past four years. Granted, Marcus may have been dead wrong for getting caught up in his personal agenda, but that's what made him the star that he was. Being a slacker now certainly wasn't going to get him into the mayoral office down the line, and Sydney was all about the big picture. When Martin Luther King was busy leading the masses, he probably missed more than a movie date with Coretta.

Sydney checked her cell, then paused to reconsider. Instead of calling and simply saying she forgave him, she decided that after choir practice, she would go over to his house and show him all evening long.

6
LAUREN

"I told my parents we went to Harry's and a late movie last night — be aware," Donald told Lauren as she helped him get ready in the choir room for practice at the Grace Temple AME Church of Christ.

"Ooh, out biting pillows again?" she asked as she pulled a lint brush over the shoulders of his choir robe.

"The dancing queen's got jokes, huh?" he laughed. "So, was that your ass I saw bouncing next to Young Jeezy's head in his latest video?"

"You actually noticed a girl's body part while you were drooling over Jeezy?"

Donald chuckled, picking imaginary dirt from his perfectly manicured nails. This was the running joke between Lauren and her kinda-sorta boyfriend, whom — despite all glaring signs to the contrary — everyone mistakenly believed was straight. After all, in Atlanta, one gay guy's effeminate behavior could easily be the next cultured Southern boy's charm. But Donald and Lauren kept up appearances because each was the other's perfect alibi for all their dirty little deeds. For Donald, Lauren was a beard that he wore as often as he found himself down at the AU, making the acquaintance of some of those cute, intellectual college boys. For Lauren? Well, to keep Keisha and Altimus in check, Donald was the perfect alibi: smart, nonthreatening, gentlemanly, from good stock. And whenever one of Lauren's boy toys thought he was going to get a little more from Lauren than she was willing to put out, all she had to do was reference her "boyfriend" to get them to back off.

It was a match made in heaven.

"Anyway," Donald said, "how'd it go at the video shoot?"

"Never mind the video shoot," Lauren snapped. "Some other stuff went down and I need to figure out . . ."

Just then, Tonya Giddens belted out a high note, totally interrupting Lauren's train of thought. Lauren's head snapped back; she scowled. So did Donald.

"Ugh, must she be so loud? It's not like she needs to draw more attention to herself with that back-to-Africa afro she keeps forcing on the rest of us," Donald said. "I thought Madame C. J. Walker created a remedy for that mess back in the forties. Guess Tonya didn't get the memo." He let out a howl that made a few of the choir members, Sydney included, look in their direction. Sydney cut her eyes at Lauren from across the piano.

"Uh-oh. The African princess is glaring," Donald said, jutting his chin in Sydney's direction. "Guess she don't like you dissing Tonya's coif."

Lauren rolled her eyes, turned her back to her sister, and ran her fingers through her silky shoulder-length weave. "Seriously, I'm in no mood to get into it with her about her back-to-the-motherland stance on hair this afternoon, and particularly her decision to stalk the earth looking like her thick, curly bush of a head ain't seen a comb, like, ever. I mean, I would straight take a razor to my wrist if Jamilah couldn't find her way from Snellville to Buckhead every other week to fry, dye, and lay my hair to the side."

The two sisters locked eyes, neither willing to look away. Suddenly, Sydney walked toward her sister. Lauren braced herself for Miss Nappy Roots to start up their running argument about how she and the rest of the good light-skinned folks of their circle were backward. But Sydney just walked on by, and stalked out the door.

"What's up with your sister?" Donald asked, confused.

"Who cares? If it's not one thing, it's another with her. But whatever. Check it, I got a serious problem," Lauren said, leaning in to Donald.

"Well, damn, I guess so, with you and your sister looking like you're about to throw bows," he said.

"It's not about her. I got a phone call the other day from my father."

"So, what'd he say? You better pull up your grades and panties if you want that inheritance?" Donald laughed as he grabbed Lauren by the hand and walked over to the full-length mirror to check out his robe.

"No, not Altimus, jackass — my *real* father, Dice Jackson."

"What? I thought he was locked under the jail!" Donald frowned, staring at Lauren's reflection in the mirror.

"He was," Lauren said, looking into Donald's eyes. The night Donald had come clean to Lauren about his homosexuality, Lauren had given him the 411 on her father, the jailbird. He knew all the dirty details, but, friend that he was, Donald never told anyone — not even Dara knew about the Duke family history. "He's out now."

"Damn, word? And he called you? Your moms know 'bout this?"

"Hell, no — if she does, she didn't get it from me. If Keisha Duke knew Dice was back in Atlanta and trying to see us, she'd flip right back to her days in the West End, cock Altimus's gun, and shoot him her damn self."

"It's like that?" Donald asked.

"It's like that."

"So what he want?"

"He wants to see me and Sydney. And she's all pressuring me to do it. We got into it Friday, so I'm assuming she's mad about it."

"But you're not going, right? I mean, if your moms found out —"

"Who cares what my mother thinks?" Lauren shot back. "In case you haven't noticed, I don't really give a crap whether Keisha likes what I'm doing or not — even if she thinks I do. Fact of the matter is, he's back in town, and I need to figure out if I want to see what he's talking about now, or if I want him to go away. That's my decision, not my mom's, not Sydney's."

"Fine," Donald said, slightly annoyed. "But you know she'll be in that ass if she finds out you was talkin' to Dice."

"Whatever . . ." Lauren said, turning her attention to her reflection in the mirror. She adjusted her choir robe so that her diamond-encrusted cross fell perfectly between her breasts. As she began to run her fingers through her silky hair, Donald elbowed her out of the way. *What the hell?*

"Whatever, whatever," Donald whispered over his shoulder as he struck his own *GQ* poses directly in front of Lauren. "Obviously, you got a mouth on you, but Keisha ain't no joke . . ."

"Um, what the hell are you doing?" Lauren said, going from annoyed to pissed in seconds flat. She put her hands on

60

her hips and was just about to go off on Donald for blocking her view when the choral director, a white guy named Ron Sheff who just loved the Lord, chamber music, and choir boys (in that order), cleared his throat to get everyone's attention. "People! Hello!" Ron said with a clap of his hands. "It's time. Soloists first, choir en masse second!"

"Okay, darling. Gotta run," Donald said, turning to reach toward Lauren to give her a peck on the lips. His face met with her fistful of Altoids instead.

"Mint?" she said in disgust, unable to contain herself. "'Cause your ass needs it. Ever get around to having that checked out?" It was all she could do not to remind Donald for the hundredth time that he needed to make an appointment with someone to see if everything on his insides was right, because his chronic halitosis made it extremely difficult for her to even have a conversation with him, much less fake-tongue him down to keep up their PDA charades.

"Whatever, bitch," Donald said, pushing the Altoids away and awkwardly taking Lauren's shoulders into his hands to pull her closer. He stuck his tongue into her mouth and wiggled it and his head around, throwing in a few "mm-MM's" for emphasis. Lauren fell out laughing at his dramatics, which left a few of the other choir members shaking their heads.

"You're the one," he said, twirling out the door.

Lauren shook her head; just as she was about to follow the choir out of the room, her Sidekick rang. She snatched it out of her purse, pounded the answer button, and practically yelled a much-annoyed "Hello?"

"Yeah, Lauren? This is Hal Workman, down at Paintless Dent Removal. Calling you about your Saab."

"Oh, yeah, hey," Lauren said, adjusting her voice. She'd been anxious to hear from him and hoping he'd have some good news about the repairs to her car. As usual, she needed him to be quick about it because she hadn't exactly told her parents she was in a car accident in the first place. She'd talked Will, one of the sales guys at Altimus's Conyers dealership, to let her "borrow" a loaner identical to her Saab while she got Baby fixed, and she needed to get that loaner back to Conyers before Altimus noticed it was missing, or worse, before he noticed that the car parked in his driveway wasn't really Lauren's.

"How's it going, Hal? Did you fix my baby? Can I come pick it up today?"

"I'm sorry, Lauren, but Mr. Duke came down to the shop earlier on some business and saw your Saab here. He asked me to put it in storage. I just thought I'd give you a head's up and let you know I won't be at Paintless anymore," Hal said, his voice dark.

"You won't be at Paintless anymore? What . . ."

"You didn't think your father would eventually catch on to what I've been doing for you? In case you were wondering, he wasn't a happy camper knowing I was helping you deceive him. So my boss fired me. Just wanted to call and tell you to have a nice life."

"Oh, God, Hal, I'm so —"

Lauren's apology was cut off by a dial tone. She silently cursed to herself; Altimus hadn't let on that he knew about the accident or the loaner car when she and Lauren left for practice. He was probably home waiting for her ass, figuring out a way to punish her for real. For sure, this one probably would be worse than the time she and Sydney took the cherry red Sting Ray coupe — one of twelve in his classic car collection — for a spin to Lake Lanier sans his permission. He had called them everything but a child of God when they pulled back into the driveway with his ride, and then not only proceeded to bar them from driving their own cars for a month, but relegated them to calling a car service and begging rides from their friends (taking MARTA, Atlanta's ridiculously inadequate commuter train system, was so not an option — the thing didn't go past Stone Mountain, for Christ's sake. And besides, it was gross — that much Lauren knew from riding on it once). Thank God Dara and Donald could shuttle her around, but it was still a major pain to have to depend on others for rides.

Lauren put her Sidekick on vibrate and pushed it back into her purse, then walked out into the sanctuary. Though at any given choir practice she could find herself in a compromising position with one of her side pieces in her cuddle corner (really, it was a small closet just off the pastor's office), she didn't often find herself on her knees in the Grace Temple AME Church of Christ. But today, she decided, she was going to have to do a little kneeling on that pulpit to ask God to save her ass from Altimus.

7
SYDNEY

"Hey, Lauren," Sydney called across the hall to her sister's room, "Lau-ren!"

"What?" was the grumpy response she finally received.

"Would you do me a favor?"

"No."

"Lauren, I'm serious." Sydney gritted her teeth against the sound of her sister's voice.

"So am I. Leave me alone," Lauren replied in the same annoyed tone of voice.

Sighing, Sydney walked over to Lauren's room. "Lauren, it will take two seconds."

"God, Syd, what part of 'no' don't you get?" Lauren questioned from a very comfortable-looking spot on the middle of her extra-deep queen-size bed. "Besides, after that shit you pulled about *you know who* — trying to guilt me into going to see him. Man, please."

"I *get* what you said. For the record, nobody's trying to guilt you into anything, I just thought you should know. Besides, you're the last person that should be telling me no to anything considering I'm the one with the car you'll need to borrow while you're on punishment. Again," Sydney said, referring to the two-hour, high-decibel chew-out Lauren got from Altimus as soon as they walked in from rehearsal for getting into a car accident and using the guys at Paintless to cover her tracks. Sydney tried desperately to make Altimus understand that his supposed punishment for Lauren — that she be "forced" to share Sydney's ride until she could appreciate having and taking care of her own — was really a punishment for her, too. But Altimus was too pissed to bow to logic. Which Sydney thought was some straight bull. "I'm just saying, you'd think a girl would be grateful — or at least scared — the car she needs to drive will be unavailable to her when she needs it."

Sydney turned around and walked back to her room. By the time she counted to twenty-one, Lauren was standing in her doorway. "Okay, what do you need me to do?"

"Can you please take me over to Marcus's house?"

"Are you serious? Why can't you drive or have him scoop you up? I don't need the car."

"Because I want to surprise him when he gets home from

66

volunteering at the Boys Club, and that won't happen if he sees my car in his driveway."

"Fine, whatever." Lauren answered matter-of-factly. "I guess I could use a Ben & Jerry's sundae to relieve the tension in my temples anyhow."

"From all the stress of Altimus up in your face, I'm sure," Syd mumbled.

"What'd you just say?"

"Nothing. Just hurry up and get ready."

"Yeah, that's what I thought," Lauren said with a roll of her eyes as she turned to head back into her room. "I'll be ready in thirty minutes or so."

Almost an hour later, Lauren emerged from her room dressed in a skintight Pucci minidress, purple Prada slingback pumps, and a huge pair of Nicole Richie-esque Christian Dior sunglasses propped on her head, looking like she was headed to Club 112 instead of on a quick sundae run. With only a curt head-nod, Lauren indicated to Sydney that she was ready. It took all of Sydney's strength not to gag.

"By the time we get there, he'll already be home," Sydney seethed through clenched teeth as she buckled up the seat belt on the passenger side of her car.

"Whatever, I don't even understand why you're going out of your way for Marcus anyway," Lauren replied as she pulled out of the driveway. "Ain't he already your man?"

"Of course you wouldn't understand, Lauren. The only other person you know how to be nice to besides yourself is your sidekick, Dara."

"Humph, at least I know I can depend on Dara to be faithful!" Lauren fired back.

"Excuse you? What's that supposed to mean?"

For a fleeting second, Lauren contemplated 'fessing up to the scene she had witnessed at the High. But one glance at the indignant look in Sydney's eyes at the mere mention of Marcus's potential shortcomings and she quickly changed her mind. "Nothing. Nothing. If you want to waste a perfectly good Saturday night waiting around for your way jabber-jaw, power-to-the-people, fake Rasta, wannabe politician boyfriend, have fun. I could care less," Lauren stated as she turned up the radio and simultaneously drowned out the remainder of the conversation.

By the time they pulled up to Marcus's lavish colonial-style home, Lauren was talking a mile a minute on her cell phone about some stripe on the new cheerleading uniforms and Sydney's head was killing her. Thanking God for small favors, Sydney jumped out of the car. "Thanks," she offered lamely as she straightened the green-and-white-striped Ella Moss top that Marcus loved so much.

Without a word, Lauren reversed out of the driveway at top speed. Sydney inhaled deeply and walked toward the front door.

The sound of the doorbell was drowned out by the incessant barking of Ms. Green's two toy Yorkshires, Pork and Chop. "Who is it?"

"It's Sydney, Ms. Green."

The heavy oak door swung open. There was Marcus's statuesque mom, bent over and scooping up the frantic Chop. Althena Green looked exactly like an older Omarosa, except with a pair of small reading glasses. "Shh, be quiet, you!" she admonished the little noisemaker as she turned her thousand-watt smile in Sydney's direction. "Hey, honey! What a pleasant surprise! Please come inside." She gracefully stepped aside to allow Sydney to enter the bright foyer. "Do you hear these little monsters?" she asked with a laugh. "I swear I'm putting them up for sale on eBay!"

"Oh, you know you love them," Sydney chided as she stopped to scoop up Pork.

"Between you and me, sometimes more than Marcus," Althena joked as she closed the door securely behind her.

"Speaking of which, is your son home from the Boys Club movie night?"

"Um, I think the movie night was canceled because of some Jewish holiday this week. He's at some study group thing or the other. But we spoke about fifteen minutes ago and he should be home shortly."

"Great, then I can surprise him after all. Mind if I wait?"

"Of course not, dear. Go ahead to his room. If you guys

69

decide to stay in for a late dinner or even just dessert, be sure to let Belinda know."

"Thanks, Ms. Green," Sydney said, placing the squirming Pork down. She started up the wide wooden staircase.

"If you need anything, just give me a holler, ya hear?"

"Yes, ma'am."

The soft scent of Marcus's Marc Jacobs cologne enveloped Sydney as soon as she stepped into his room. She closed her eyes as the fragrance brought back warm memories of the two of them cuddled up, then she gently fingered a framed photo of them from last year's spring formal. The twists that Toni, Mrs. Duke's personal hairdresser, had put in Sydney's hair for the occasion complemented Marcus's freshly touched-up locs even better than she remembered. But Sydney was most thankful that half of her big butt was blocked from the camera's view by Marcus's towering frame.

Next her glance fell upon the open MacBook right in front of her. Hmm. She softly pressed the "on" button and the screen reopened to the AOL homepage.

She took a quick look behind her to ensure that the door was completely closed. Once Sydney was sure the coast was clear, she scrolled down the Web site history log.

Let's see: a Google search for Princeton; youngrichandtriflin.com; myspace.com; facebook.com; lots of youtube.com; nothing too out of the ordinary. Sydney clicked on his inbox to see whom he'd been e-mailing. *Hmm.* There was a fantasy football newsletter; a quick note from his boy, mikeyd2008, about some march in DC; and an alert from YRT about the latest student-body scandal. Finding nothing remarkable in the first ten, Sydney decided to check the trash folder when an unfamiliar address caught her attention. *Who was misskitty80?* As she sorted by sender, Sydney noticed at least twenty or more e-mails from the unfamiliar user ID in the trash. Sydney opened an e-mail from Thursday night:

> Hey babe just got home. SUCH a long day . . . Sorry I missed you before lunch, I was running late. But by the time I got to the cafeteria, you were already eating. It's so weird for me now when I see you with her. Oh, well. Can't wait for our next "study session."
> X and Os, Dara

Did Dara just refer to my boyfriend as "babe"? Sydney scanned through all the others; every single one of them was as personal as the last. In all the discussions about his difficult class load, Marcus never once mentioned having classes with Dara, let alone her being his study partner. And exactly what did she mean by "it's so weird for me *now*"? Just then, she heard the sound of a car pulling up into the driveway. Sydney quickly closed the e-mail and shut down the site. She rushed over to the window and stood behind the curtain.

Wait a minute — why did that cherry-red Audi look so familiar? Sydney moved slightly to get a better view of the driver of the car in the dim driveway light. It was Dara! What the hell was her sister's best friend doing driving Marcus home? How much damn studying were they doing together?

While Sydney stood there struggling to figure it out, Marcus leaned over and gave Dara a quick peck on the cheek. He jumped out, waved good-bye, and headed inside. She could hear him call out in greeting to his mom and even Belinda, the housekeeper, as he stomped up the stairs. Sydney rushed back over to the bed and tried to compose herself.

"Hey, what are you doing here? Everything okay?" Marcus exclaimed in surprise, as he opened the door to find Sydney sitting on the edge of the bed reading one of his issues of *GQ*. She couldn't tell if his smile was genuine or a knee-jerk reaction to the shock of finding her unsupervised in his room.

"Sure. I figured I'd come over and surprise you," Sydney responded as she fought to remain calm. She refused to jump to any conclusions and risk trashing four years' worth of a relationship.

"I'm totally surprised," Marcus continued as he crossed the room in several long strides and pulled Sydney up to her feet. "Since I didn't hear from you all day, I thought you were still mad about last night." Marcus gave her a tight hug and a kiss on the cheek. When he finally released her, Sydney discreetly wiped her cheek.

"Yeah, well, you did leave me standing outside in the middle of the night while you were supposedly studying," Sydney hinted as she backed away and turned toward his desk.

"What do you mean *supposedly* studying? What else would I've been doing?"

"I don't know, Marcus, I'm just saying. You've never gotten so caught up in studying that you've forgotten me before . . ."

Marcus gently turned Sydney around. "Syd, I don't know where all these weird questions are coming from but you have to believe me, I have no reason to lie about where I was." Marcus leaned in and gave Sydney a gentle kiss on the lips to which she barely responded. *The same lips you just used to kiss Dara*, she thought bitterly.

"So lemme ask you this, since when have you and Dara been hanging out?"

For a brief second, Marcus Green looked like a deer caught in headlights . . . but only for a second. "What are you talking about?"

"Well that was her car that you just got out of, was it not?"

"We weren't hanging out, we were studying," he responded defensively, pushing his locs away from his face.

"I been told you that Dara was in my Advanced Placement Biology class." He walked past Sydney and started to straighten the already neat desktop.

"No, you didn't," Sydney insisted, refusing to back down. "And you definitely never mentioned that you'd be studying with her."

"Sydney, you're being ridiculous. Today is like the first time we've even gotten together." Marcus sighed in annoyance. "Do you have your period? 'Cause you're acting really insecure and emotional. I mean not for nothing, I don't have to tell you about every single person that I spend time with."

"Excuse me?" Sydney asked in disbelief as she remembered the e-mail that clearly implied that they'd been together before. "Are you really telling me that this is the first time you've been hanging out with Dara?" Sydney looked at Marcus as if he had just grown a third eye.

"Yes. Why, who said they saw us together? I mean I don't know what your sister may have told you about that night at the High but . . ."

Sydney didn't even hear the remainder of his sentence. Granted, she kinda figured Marcus might lie about being with Dara last night to avoid getting into another argument about leaving her stranded, but now he was talking about being seen by Lauren at the High? The event at the High Museum happened over two months ago! And just what the hell had

Lauren seen and not bothered to tell her about? Suddenly her sister's ominous comment in the car started to make too much sense. As much as she couldn't stand Lauren's trifling ways, Sydney would definitely let Lauren know if her so-called boyfriend was playing her out. I mean they were sisters, for goodness sake! Humph, so much for blood being thicker than water. . . . Just wait till she caught up with Lauren's backstabbing behind!

Like Dr. Jekyll and Mr. Hyde, Marcus again completely switched gears. "Look, babe, if you don't want me studying with her I won't. I don't want you to ever question my behavior. It's nothing. . . ."

Sydney was quiet as she considered his words. On one hand Marcus had never given Sydney any reason to worry about him liking another girl, let alone cheating on her. What had Rhea called them? The Black Ken and Barbie . . . On the other hand, he had blatantly lied about how many times he and Dara had been together. If it was really "nothing," then why lie? But then again, everyone knew that Dara was a total hoochie, just like her notorious mom, who'd tricked that poor Atlanta Falcon into getting her pregnant and now lived the high life off his generous child-support payments. Marcus was such a stickler for keeping up appearances, would he really risk it all for *Dara*?

Marcus walked over and softly fingered Sydney's shirt. "You know I don't like it when you get mad at me."

Every rational bone in her body told her to march through the door and not look back, but her heart desperately wanted to believe his words. Breathing became physically painful as she remembered Carmen and Rhea's stinging accusations from the other night. Was her strong-black-woman stance nothing but talk? "I just don't like the secrets, Marcus," she started, struggling for the words to express how she felt without seeming like she was some paranoid, insecure girlfriend.

"I would never purposely keep anything from you, Syd," he quickly assured her with soft kisses to her lips. "It won't happen again. Promise."

Even though she heard Marcus's apologetic words and saw the look of remorse on his face, something deep in Sydney's gut told her differently. And Sydney Duke's gut was rarely wrong.

8
LAUREN

"U-G-L-Y / You ain't got no alibi, you ugly / Yeah, yeah, you ugly!"

Lauren tossed her ponytail extra hard in the direction of the opposing dance team's bench and then put a little twist in her hips for good measure. Their football team was for crap on this warm Monday night — the scoreboard said they were down by fourteen points — but that was no reason to slouch on the field. Halftime was game time, and the hundred-member marching band had just tore up Luda's "Pimpin' All Over the World," putting the stale-ass St. John's All Saints Catholic High School band, with their wack traditional marching-band ditties, to absolute shame. And since all eyes were on Lauren Duke, she was making every effort to make bitches — and their boyfriends, of course — remember exactly who she was.

"Damn, girl — if you shook it any harder, it might have fallen off," Marvin Joyce yelled out to Lauren as she passed by him. When she looked him in the face, he winked.

"And you'd be right there to pick it up, wouldn't you, Marvin?" Lauren shot back. "Too bad I read on YRT that Pam says you wouldn't know what to do with it, though."

Everyone on his bleacher and several more surrounding it fell out in hysterics. "Ooh, she got you," one guy shouted. "Pick up that lip, bruh," said another.

Lauren smiled and bounced back to the dance-squad seats. The actual game bored her to tears, but she loved the spirit of it — how everyone dressed in the school colors and chanted alongside the squad when the girls were performing. The dance squad was God at Brookhaven Prep, even if the football team made a point of embarrassing the mess out of them by losing every other game, today's included.

"Well, despite the loss, it's still good to be the queen," Lauren announced to her squad. "Don't forget, JV is having a bake sale tomorrow to raise money for the senior squad members' homecoming breakfast. Maria, make sure they come correct, right? I will send them steppin' if they're wack, bringing out some bran muffins or something."

Dara laughed as she tossed up a high five.

"And whose mom was responsible for the snacks today? Um, carrots and dip? What, are we in pre-K? You skinny things could stand a steak or two to fill out these uniforms properly. And you all should know by now that in order for me to dance at full capacity, I need my sugar and carbs. Don't play. Dismissed."

"Damn, is that Ebony over there staring all up in fine-ass Cole's face?" Dara interrupted, as she leaned into Lauren and pointed four bleachers back. Lauren squinted her eyes to take in a better view; indeed, that scabby trick was all up on her next conquest. Lauren had thought she'd made her intentions clear to him at the pregame rally, when she'd sized him up and decided he'd be the perfect accessory when she accepted her homecoming-queen crown. Clearly, he needed it spelled out. "Damn sure is."

Just as Lauren got up from the bleachers to make her next move on Cole, her Sidekick went off. She looked to see who it was but didn't recognize the number. "Hello?" she shouted into the mouthpiece.

"Lauren?" a deep but unsure voice questioned on the other end.

"Who's this?" she said with even more attitude as she detoured from her original mission, rounded the corner of the big brick football field gate, and stepped closer to Sydney's silver Saab, Dara in tow.

"It's Jermaine," he said, this time with much more confidence.

"Jermaine? Jermaine who?"

"Jermaine from the West End — you know, the brother you crashed into?"

Hold up! The cute boy from the West End? How'd he get her number? Better yet, who the hell told him he could use it?

"Right, right, the service call . . ." Lauren said, turning to Dara to mouth a good-bye. "That still doesn't explain how you got this number."

"Let's just say a brotha got skills." He laughed. "You told me if I got the digits, I could call. So I got the digits. Don't worry about how. And by the way, baby blue on silver is definitely working for you."

Lauren looked down at her uniform as if she didn't know what color it was; her heart did a flip when she realized he'd seen her. Here. This evening. But where was he?

"Look up," he said.

"What?" she said as she fumbled for the keys.

"Look. Up."

She did. And there he was, on the hill overlooking the parking lot. Cutie from the West End. Live and in the flesh. She took a quick look around to see if anyone was paying attention. Damn, he was fine.

"What are you doing here?" she said into the phone, unsure whether she should smile or hang up and call 911 to report him as a stalker.

"Let's just say I like football and Brookhaven's halftime

show — or, more specifically, a certain cheerleader on the varsity squad who performed in it," Jermaine said as he walked up to the car.

Lauren didn't say anything. She just blushed.

"Anyway, you made it hard for a fan to concentrate, bouncing all over the field like that in that short skirt," Jermaine continued. "And seeing as you banged up my ride and all, I think you owe me something."

"But I've already arranged for you to get it fixed." Playa found her number and her school, too. She knew it was that damn Hal. If he still worked at Paintless, she would have smacked him upside his head. Of course, she might have to track him down to thank him, depending on what the boy had to say next.

They were standing face-to-face now but still talking into their cell phones.

"I wanted to say thank you like the gentleman you demanded I be when we first met. Why don't you let me take you out for dinner Friday night? I'll pick you up."

"Awfully cocky of you to drive all the way from the West End to Brookhaven Prep to hook up with the head cheerleader and expect I'll just say yes," Lauren snapped, closing her cellphone.

"Uh, awfully cocky of you to assume that the only reason someone from the West End would come here is to see you," Jermaine snapped back, staring into her eyes without so much as a flinch. He snapped his CRAZR closed. "Look," he said, taking a breath, "it may sound corny, but I think you hitting my car happened for a reason, and I can't get you off my mind."

Lauren giggled. She could feel her heart skipping a few beats as she considered, even if for a moment, what it would be like to be wrapped in his arms. But wasn't no way he was coming to the Duke house — at least not while Lauren's parents were home.

After staring into his sexy eyes for a beat, Lauren decided to let him take her out. "Sure. But I'll meet you there," she said, fiddling with her keys.

The rattle of the keys made Jermaine look at Sydney's car. "Damn, your daddy didn't waste no time getting you a new ride, huh?"

"Actually, that's my sister's car," Lauren said. She quickly decided she didn't want to get into details with him on the torture Altimus had exacted on her for getting into her last wreck. "Mine is, um, still in the shop. How about you meet me at Lenox Mall? We could grab a bite to eat and maybe check out a movie. Let's say, eight-thirty sharp?"

He leaned in and kissed her cheek ever so softly with those juicy lips. "Don't be late," he whispered, and then swaggered toward his car. He tugged his hoodie over his head to stave off the early evening chill. Lauren watched him, grinning, until he disappeared into the raw Atlanta sunset.

9
SYDNEY

"Oh, my God, I almost forgot to tell you! So remember that guy I told you about? The one I met the other day while I was in the golf-pro shop looking for my dad's birthday gift? Well he *finally* called me," Carmen blurted out as soon as the end of period bell sounded. "Do you think it's a bad sign that it took him two days?"

"Is that so . . ." Sydney replied simply as she stood and gathered her English Lit books from her desk. Although Sydney normally enjoyed hearing all the juicy details of her best friends' boy escapades, she was still way too stressed out from the whole Marcus and Dara situation to serve up meaningful relationship advice at the moment. Add to the equation that she was now being forced to chauffeur around the same trifling-ass twin that essentially conspired to sabotage her relationship and Sydney felt on the verge of a straightjacket-worthy meltdown. The only thing stopping her from checking into the nearest rehab facility was the anticipation of seeing Dice again. When he called on Sunday night, they made plans for her to try to swing by after school that week if she could get out of debate-team practice.

"Sydney! Did you not hear a word I just said?" Carmen questioned a little too sharply for Sydney's taste as she stopped dead in her tracks. "You're not still mad about what happened after the last committee meeting? 'Cause I mean seriously, you know Rhea didn't mean — "

"Carmen, please. I am not even thinking about Rhea's over-the-top theatrics."

"So then, what's wrong with you? You didn't return any of my calls all weekend, yesterday you weren't in school, and you've been like, absolutely mute all day today," Carmen insisted, obviously unwilling to budge until Sydney came clean about her funny attitude.

Sighing, Sydney readjusted her new gold-mirrored Louis Vuitton doctor's bag on her forearm while making a mental note not to forget to follow up with her guidance counselor about scheduling an advanced SAT tutorial into her schedule for next semester. "Girl, it was just like, the longest weekend ever. I needed a day to get my life together. Lauren crashed her car AGAIN."

"Again! What is this, her third accident this week?"

"Seems like it, right? But wait, that's just the beginning. Apparently Einstein tried to cover up the accident by replacing her car with an identical loaner while it was being repaired in the shop. Except Altimus totally found out — like he always does.

"Shut. Up. I know he was so pissed . . ." Carmen's eyes widened like saucers.

"Can I just tell you? Altimus is worse than freaking CSI; nothing gets past that man. He hit the roof when we got home from choir practice. Lauren was hemmed up in his study for at least two hours straight. I swear, she was Kunta Kinte and he was the slave master. Which, honestly, didn't bother me at all until the part where he decided to revoke Lauren's car privileges for the next month."

"A month? What is she going to do without a car for a month?"

"According to Altimus, learn how to share."

"Huh? I'm confused."

"It just occurred to my stepfather that the reason Lauren continues to crash her car is because she's been spoiled into believing that the world revolves around her. So to teach her a lesson, she will have to share a car with the rest of us in the house. Since Lauren no longer has her own car and neither of my parents are even about to let her come within fifty feet of theirs, I have to share my car with Lauren. Which is why I took a mental health day yesterday."

"And with Homecoming around the corner, too? Whew, your stepfather was too thorough with Lauren." Carmen shook her head in disbelief.

"So basically, it's about to be all about 'Driving Ms. Lauren' unless I want her behind the wheel of my car."

"Humph, no wonder you're having a moment," Carmen mused as the two finally joined the procession of students headed toward the cafeteria. "And your mom didn't say anything in your defense?"

"Oh, please, if you think my mom is about to get into an argument with Altimus over *my* car situation, you're very mistaken. Now then, if she was the one who had to drive Lauren around, it might be a different story."

Before Carmen could further sympathize, Rhea rushed over from the opposite end of the hall. "My God, Mr. Hicks is a total maniac," she complained animatedly, oblivious to Sydney and Carmen's somber demeanors. "I just took my fifth pop quiz since the school year started what, two months ago? Jesus H. Christ!"

"Really? I guess that means we'll be getting one from him after lunch, huh?" Carmen questioned.

"Pretty much," Rhea replied as the three girls stopped at Rhea's locker just shy of the entrance to the cafeteria. All three put their textbooks inside and quickly straightened out their respective outfits in her locker mirror. Finally noticing

Sydney's silence, Rhea turned to face her. "What's wrong with you?

"Nothing worth talking about," Sydney answered. "The regular Lauren dramatics ruining my life."

"Okay . . ." Rhea hesitated.

"You know, Syd, I meant to tell you earlier how cute your skirt is today. BCBG?" Carmen immediately attempted to steer the conversation in a more neutral direction.

"Actually it's Theory, but thanks. I picked it up a couple of weeks ago at Nordstrom. I was worried that it made my thighs look a little big, but it was marked down almost half off so I couldn't pass it up. What do you guys think?" Sydney turned slightly so her friends could scrutinize the knee-length brown A-line skirt with pink-ribbon detail that complemented her cream top.

"Absolutely not. You look adorable," Carmen assured.

"You're so good," Rhea confirmed as she slammed the locker door and twisted the purple-faced Master Lock one last time for good measure.

Sydney allowed a small smile to cross her face. Her friends always knew the right things to say to make her feel better. If only Carmen or Rhea had been born her sister, there was no way either of the two would've cosigned on some skanky loser trying to come on to Marcus. Sydney struggled to keep her mouth shut about the cryptic messages from Dara on Marcus's computer. As much as she trusted her girls, there was no way Sydney was about to let on to anyone that her boyfriend might be cheating on her. Like Dice always asserted, if you don't want it to be, don't even speak it into being. "You guys ready? I'm totally starving to death."

As usual, the activity in the cafeteria bordered on organized pandemonium. Out of the three separate lunch periods during the school day, third period was always rowdiest. In one corner the jocks horsed around loudly and entertained the giggling dance-squad members with antics that occasionally included harassing the tech geeks who sat huddled together discussing the latest high-speed gadget they planned to use their allowances to purchase. In the opposite corner, the future Black Republicans of America pretended that they were a "different kind of black people" from the tight-knit circle of young men wearing baggy jeans and the latest Billionaire Boys Club T-shirts engaged in a particularly heated rhyme battle. Drama club members predictably rocked their uniform head-to-toe black attire like a badge of honor as they shared a table beside the large-windowed wall with the members of the band. The distinct smell of weed and days-old smoke assaulted Sydney's nostrils as she made her way past the table of sleepy-looking stoners. A heavyset lunch monitor with a tacky auburn weave and serious attitude problem named Miz Bea wandered slowly between the various tables throwing dirty looks and threats of after-school detention toward any individual who seemed on the verge of cutting up.

"I already know Sydney is having her usual extra-large, strawberry, banana, and wheat-germ smoothie, but what about you, Rhea?" Carmen asked as the girls made their way toward the tower of food trays.

"Depends. My bathroom scale says a chicken-salad wrap, but I must say those Tater Tots are calling my name . . ."

"You are so damn ghetto, talking about the Tater Tots calling your name," Carmen giggled. "You know you need to back away from the deep fryer."

"I know, I know," Rhea answered remorsefully. "I just can't help myself."

"Please try," Sydney said playfully as she passed trays to Rhea and then Carmen. "Next thing, you'll be requesting smothered chicken, red Kool-Aid, and a side of watermelon."

"Hey! I happen to love smothered chicken and watermelon," Carmen asserted as they reached the serving area.

"And yet, we love you anyway, Carm," said Sydney.

"Whatever." Carmen laughed good-naturedly as she examined the expiration dates on the various flavors of yogurt.

When the three finally finished collecting their respective lunches — a health shake for Sydney; yogurt, turkey sandwich, and Perrier for Carmen; and a wrap with Vitamin Water for

Rhea — the girls headed over to their table in the very center of the cafeteria.

"So I was telling Sydney that the boy from the golf-pro shop finally called me," Carmen told Rhea.

"Sweet," Rhea responded as she stopped to grab napkins and straws.

"We shall see. He wants to hang out on Saturday afternoon. I was kinda hoping that we could all swing by the mall after school so I can try to find something to wear . . ."

"I'm in. What about you Sydney?" Rhea chirped. "Syd? Hello, Earth to Sydney . . ."

Once again, Sydney was completely distracted from the conversation around her. But this time she was far from spacing out. In fact, her attention was completely focused on what appeared to the uninformed eye to be a casual conversation between Sydney's boyfriend and her sister's best friend. "Um, sure. I'm down. You guys ready to sit?" Rhea and Carmen barely had time to reply before Sydney was halfway across the cafeteria and all the way up in Dara's face.

"I'm sorry, I'm not interrupting anything here am I?" Sydney questioned innocently as she inserted herself between Marcus and Dara on the table bench by discreetly elbowing Dara in her side.

"Oh, hey, Sydney! I didn't even see you come in the café," Marcus explained uneasily as he scooted farther away than necessary from Dara and turned toward the still-standing Rhea and Carmen. "Hey, ladies."

"Hey, y'all," Dara offered lamely as she now teetered precariously on the edge of the short bench for two.

"Hey," Carmen and Rhea replied in unison as they walked around to the empty side of the table and assumed their regular seats.

"Well, it's no wonder you didn't see us, what with Dara all up in your face like that, sweetie," Sydney continued in a deceptively cheerful tone as she picked up one of the many straws on Rhea's tray and pulled it out of the paper wrapper. Rhea's eyes bulged as Carmen gasped audibly.

"Well, then, on that note I think I'll head back over to my table . . ." Dara said, as she quickly stood up to leave the table.

"Yes, why don't you?" Sydney finished with a sneer. "Unless, of course, there's something that you'd like to share with *all* of us?" She looked at Dara expectantly.

"Have a nice lunch, Marcus," Dara huffed as she retreated back across the room to the dance squad's table.

Carmen, Rhea, and Marcus sat in shocked silence as Sydney took a long pull from her shake and looked across the table innocently. "What's wrong with you guys?"

"Nothing, *nada*," Carmen and Rhea replied, starting to eat their respective lunches as if their very lives depended on it.

Marcus cleared his throat, "So, yeah, me and Dara were just talking about the exam that we have next week."

"Is that so?" Sydney questioned as she stared Marcus down. In between bites, Carmen and Rhea discreetly exchanged looks of disbelief. In four years, they had never once seen Sydney so much as disagree with Marcus, let alone talk smack to him in the middle of the café.

"Uh, yeah. And I was just telling her that because of a conflict in my schedule she was probably gonna have to find someone else to study with from now on."

"Hmm, that's unfortunate for her. We all know Dara's not really the brightest," Sydney said without breaking her steely gaze.

In response, Marcus tugged at the French cuffs of his white-and-blue-striped Brooks Brothers button-up. "I'm sure she'll be all right," he mumbled.

Just then, Jason and a couple of teammates strolled past en route to the jocks' table. Jason slowed down as he reached Sydney's back. "Hey, Syd, what's good?" Jason said with a smile as he lightly brushed Sydney's shoulders to get her attention.

"Oh, hey, Jason. How you doing?" Sydney turned from Marcus and stood up to offer Jason a hug and a smile. She barely suppressed a laugh as she imagined the look on Marcus's face.

"You know, 'bout to get my grub on," he continued easily, as if unaware of the three sets of eyes blazing holes in his face.

"Well, let me not get in your way then," Sydney retorted playfully, stepping back.

"True, true. I'll holler at you later," he said, and with a quick general head nod at the entire table, Jason was gone.

As soon as Sydney could sit back down, Rhea jumped all over her. "Well, excuse me. I didn't know you knew Jason," she teased good-naturedly as Carmen raised her eyebrows suggestively at his retreating back. "You holding out on us now?"

"Yeah, Syd. Since when are you and Jason Darden so tight?" Marcus seethed.

"What can I say? You'd be surprised at the things that I know," Sydney hinted slyly.

"Is that so?" Marcus struggled to keep his voice even as he noticed Carmen and Rhea watching the couple go back and forth, like Venus and Serena at the final round of the US Open. "'Cause this one's news to me, too."

Sydney pretended not to hear Marcus's last comment and instead focused on her girls. "So anyway, Rhea, you were saying that Mr. Hicks was giving out pop quizzes?"

"Uh-huh." Rhea replied between sips of her Vitamin Water.

"Hmm, well, in that case, you all will have to excuse me. I was way too stressed out this weekend to get any studying done. I'm gonna go grab my notebook and try to squeeze in a last-minute review 'fore the bell rings," Sydney announced as she rose from the table with her bag and turned to walk away.

"Did you hear me, Syd?" Marcus countered, obviously frustrated as he stood up and grabbed her arm.

Sydney turned and shrugged him off with her fakest smile. "My bad. I didn't realize that I had to inform you of everyone I hang out with." Marcus paused with his mouth slightly agape. "Hmm . . . sound familiar, Marcus?" Sydney asked.

And with that, she walked away.

10
LAUREN

Lauren had checked the time on her Sidekick no less than a half dozen times by the time Jermaine rounded the corner into the Lenox Mall Food Court. It was 8:45 P.M. He was fifteen minutes late. And despite the boy had clearly kicked up his wardrobe a notch — his pants were still sagging a little too low for Lauren's comfort, but his argyle sweater and crisp white vintage Jordans were a welcome respite from the standard white T-and-Tims thug uniform he'd rocked the two other times she'd seen him — she was hardly impressed that he kept her waiting on the wooden bench like she was some common mall rat with nowhere else to be. His pearly white smile was met with a MAC Hug Me lipstick scowl. "Um, so is there something wrong with your watch?" Lauren sneered.

Jermaine looked casually at his bare wrist and, still smiling, gave Lauren a simple: "Don't have a watch. How you doing?"

"I was fine fifteen minutes ago. You're late," Lauren said, grabbing her gold clutch and folding her arms.

"Yup, I figured as much," Jermaine said just as nonchalantly, his eyebrows raised. "I let my man borrow my car, so I took MARTA over, but you know how those trains be running."

"Actually, I don't," Lauren snapped.

"Well, the way you drive, maybe you should take a ride every now and again," he said, acknowledging Lauren's attitude by mockingly wiggling his neck. Really, Jermaine wanted to get off the subject of his car. More specifically he needed to take his mind off the events leading up to his handing over the keys to his ride. To Rodney. Who wasn't a friend but his brother. His recently-released-from-prison brother. Let's just say that it wasn't a happy homecoming; not more than ten minutes after Jermaine got to work at the MLK Community Center at West End, Rodney came strolling in, yelling over the rowdy scrimmage basketball game Jermaine was refereeing.

"Baby brotha!" Rodney called out, strolling onto the court, seemingly unaware of the rush of ten-year-olds pushing the basketball across the worn-out wooden floor. "What up, man?"

Jermaine's shoulders slumped, if only for a second, and then squared themselves as Rodney took his place in front of him. Jermaine blew his whistle. "Take five, young'uns — get you some water," he said to his team, without taking his eyes off Rodney. He let his eyes roll from the top of Rodney's lint-buzzed cornrows to the bottoms of his worn-out sneakers and then back up to his eyes. They looked tired, like those of a guy who'd led a hard-knock life. For sure, Rodney fit the bill, but it was his own doing. "Ain't no babies here, brotha," Jermaine said.

"My bad, shorty, my bad," Rodney said with a chuckle. "You right. You damn sho ain't no baby. You look good, man. It's good to see you."

Nothing from Jermaine.

"I stopped by to see Mama," Rodney continued, ignoring his little brother's shade. "See you took real good care of her."

"Somebody had to," Jermaine said, fire in his eyes.

Rodney smirked and sucked his teeth. "Yeah, little man — enough of the chitchat. Look here, Mama said you had a car. I need to ride for a minute — where the keys at?"

"Nah, man, I need my car. I got things to do tonight. Besides, don't you felons got curfews or something?" Jermaine asked coldly.

"Felons, huh?" Rodney asked as he fixed his mouth to lay into his brother. But he was cut off by Little Mike, the star of the MLK Thunderbirds, who sidled up to the two brothers midcourt, unaware of the tension that had enveloped them.

"Hey, Mr. Jermaine, I brought you some water," Little Mike said to his coach, thrusting a bottle of Crystal Springs in his face. Jermaine took the water and thanked his young charge.

"Good looking out. Why don't you go get the guys to run some drills? I'll be over in a second," Jermaine told Little Mike, who looked at Jermaine and then over to Rodney and then back at Jermaine again. Something was wrong — Little Mike could feel it.

"What up, little man," Rodney said to the boy, raising his chin in greeting.

"Hey," he said.

"Playing a little ball, huh?"

"Yeah," Little Mike said.

"Look man, go on over and run some drills like I said," Jermaine said, growing uncomfortable. He watched as Little Mike trotted off, then turned his attention back to his brother. "Listen, I need my car, man. Wherever you got to go, you need to figure out another way to get there."

"Well, I can definitely find another way to get there — you know that," Rodney said, a grin spreading across his face. "I figured I'd start out on my first week out the pen doing the right thing."

"The right thing, huh?"

"Yup, the right thing. So you gonna help your big brother out, or I need to find an alternate means of transportation?"

That, Jermaine didn't want to have any part of, considering the last time Rodney found an alternate means of transportation, it led to a multicount indictment involving a car-theft ring that spanned three states, with Rodney all up in the middle of it. Desperate to prove her son's innocence, Eugenia Watson put her house up for his bail; that fool skipped out on his first court date and left Eugenia and Jermaine holding the bag.

Jermaine looked Rodney up and down again. This, right here? He. Did. Not. Need. He reached into his gym shorts and pulled the thick ring of keys out of his pocket. He fingered them for a moment as he stared intensely into Rodney's eyes.

"Don't worry, baby brother, I'll take good care of your ride," Rodney said, slowly pulling the keys from Jermaine's grasp. He tossed them in the air and winked at his little brother, then trotted off the court, Jermaine gritting his teeth enough to make the veins in his forehead dance a jig.

Yeah, the last thing Jermaine wanted to think about was his car.

"So you gonna spend the rest of the night being mad about a few minutes you can't call back, or can a brother get a bite to eat and see a flick? Get a little conversation going? Chop it up? What?" Jermaine folded his arms; a smile smoothed easily across his face, his lips creating the perfect frame for his perfectly straight, perfectly white teeth. Lauren definitely didn't want to push the car issue anymore — no need to include Jermaine in her tragic family saga, and definitely no need to dredge up ugly memories of the verbal smackdown and stunningly harsh punishment Altimus Duke administered that she was still suffering under. Besides, she just could not resist the dimples.

"Whatever. Come on here, boy," she said, smiling slowly and standing to reveal her cuffed jean shorts, fitted red leather jacket, and beige silk Bebe camisole, an ensemble she sweated over for a good forty-five minutes before she decided it had just enough flash to make his eyes bubble. It worked.

"I ain't hardly a boy, but I'll definitely follow if you're leading," Jermaine said, slipping his hands around Lauren's waist and pulling her close to him. He planted a soft kiss on her cheek. "Hello, Ms. Duke. How are you today?"

Lauren practically melted into the patchwork of tile beneath their feet, so taken was she by this man. "Ms. Duke is just fine, thank you," Lauren said, savoring his kiss. She was about to kiss him back, but then remembered where she was: in the middle of a busy mall with hundreds of people making their way to the restaurants and movie theaters just beyond them. Though the risk was low that she'd run into somebody she knew (her friends and her mother's friends, too, tended to frequent the more upscale Phipps Plaza just down the road), didn't nobody, especially those who knew the Dukes, need to see her all booed up with Thug Passion, no matter how nice his sweater was, Lauren quickly decided as she pulled back from his embrace. "Let's walk and talk, shall we? I don't think we have time enough to sit and eat; you can buy me some popcorn after you get my movie ticket."

"So much for women's equality, huh," Jermaine teased as he took her hand into his and followed along. "I thought you independent women liked to pay your own way."

"Oh, I'm independent," Lauren insisted, smiling sweetly. "But I'm also a lady — don't you forget it."

Now Jermaine was having his whatever moment. "Okay, Ms. Lady. So, what are we going to do to kill forty minutes if you're not going to let me take you out to eat?"

Just then, Lauren's eyes zoned in on a pair of hot-pink-and-burgundy BCBG heels; her instantaneous love affair with the glorious creations made her go temporarily deaf but miraculously improved the speed of her limbs, which wasted no time dragging her, Jermaine in tow, to the window for a closer look.

"Um, okay — I guess this is your way of telling me you want to window-shop, huh?"

Window-shop? Not quite. Lauren, who treated the purchase of shoes, clothes, purses, and jewelry like it was a stealth Marine mission to liberate prisoners of war, had no intention of leaving those pumps behind. "My God, I have to have those shoes," Lauren said, her nose pressed against the window so hard that a small cloud of breath fog formed on the glass. "Just look at them. The most perfect . . . hot . . . pink . . . suede . . . shoes . . . ever. I can't breathe," she said, patting her hand on her chest.

Jermaine laughed, thinking she was being theatrical for kicks. "Must-have's, huh?" he asked, just as a saleswoman slammed down the store's gate.

"Oh, no, excuse me — can I get in real quick? I just need those shoes in size seven," Lauren said, rushing over to the entrance and knocking on the glass door.

"Sorry, we're closed," the saleswoman said, shrugging. "We're open at ten A.M. tomorrow."

"I won't be here tomorrow," Lauren fumed.

"Well, I'm sorry, but the register is shut down so you can't buy them tonight, and the store's closed," the saleswoman said as she walked away.

"Damn," Lauren said, pouting.

"Uh, you gonna be all right?" Jermaine asked, only half joking.

Lauren sucked her teeth. "I wanted those shoes. She could have just got them for me right quick."

"But the store is closed, Lauren."

"Whatever. That's why she sells shoes for a living, evil ass," Lauren huffed at the woman, but not loud enough for her to hear it, of course.

"What's that supposed to mean?" Jermaine asked, reeling back.

Lauren, lost in the moment, didn't catch on right away that she'd offended Jermaine; she was too busy mumbling under her breath about how she was going to find time in the next few days to get back to Lenox, seeing as she had dance-squad practice for Homecoming, a Homecoming Dance decorations committee meeting, and, of course, no dibs on her sister's ride.

"You know my moms used to sell shoes," Jermaine snapped.

Now *that* she heard. "Damn, my bad, Jermaine, I didn't mean anything by that."

"Of course, the shoes my moms was selling were much more practical than a pair of overpriced pink shoes that probably look a lot like all the other pink shoes you got in your closet," Jermaine continued, still fuming.

Hold up, Lauren thought — *is he dissing me? Oh, hell to the no*. "Practical? What you know about practical, with your pair of hundred-dollar tennis shoes? That look a lot like all the other tennis shoes you got in *your* closet?"

"There's a big difference between my sneakers and your shoes, trust me," Jermaine said, readjusting his tone.

"How you figure? You wear yours to get attention, and I do the same with mine," Lauren said, still upset.

"Now that's where you wrong, shawty." Jermaine

laughed. "I wear my expensive sneakers to keep attention off of me. Ain't no way I could hit the block with the cheap shit and not catch crap from the dough boys, you feel me? But you, you could be in a hoodie and jeans and ten-dollar shoes from Payless, and I'd still think you fly."

Lauren wanted to giggle, but she felt like she still needed to give him some grief for talking about her shoe game. "Boy, what you know about Payless? That's the kinda chicks you roll with?"

"Nah," Jermaine laughed nervously. "My moms shops that way — got to. 'Cause selling shoes don't exactly pay all the bills."

Lauren closed her mouth. She gave herself an imaginary kick in the ass and said a silent "damn" for good measure. Thing is, Jermaine wasn't embarrassed about this.

"I help her out a little — you know, I got this job down at the community center helping with the neighborhood kids over there. That's until I get some bigger stuff bubblin'."

Just as Lauren was trying to figure out something to say to pull them out of this extremely awkward conversation, someone shouted an "oo-oooh" call as a group of teens sidled up to them. Instinctively, Jermaine looked up and threw a hand signal at them — a gesture that made Lauren just a little nervous. She'd never, after all, dated someone who threw up what might be considered gang signs.

"Yo, what up, gangsta," one of the guys said to Jermaine, leaning in for a pound and round-the-way man hug.

"It's all good, you know," Jermaine said, massaging his chin between his forefinger and thumb. "Getting ready to go check out a flick."

"Aight then," the guy said as his friends crowded Jermaine and Lauren. One of them, a girl dressed in an ill-fitting jean jacket and stretchy jeans that looked like they'd been painted on, looked Lauren up and down like she was two seconds off of skinning her alive. "Yo, I seen your brother out on the block," the guy continued. "Glad to see he home. Lookin' all beefy and shit."

"Yeah," Jermaine said, wanting desperately to change the subject. He had no intention of explaining to Lauren where Rodney had just come from, at least not that night. "Listen, this is my girl, Lauren. Lauren, this is everybody." Lauren gave a quick wave; Jermaine's friends' response was tepid, at best. "We gotta get going — our movie's about to start."

"Aight then, nephew, we'll see you round the way," Jermaine's friend said.

"I'll get at you, man," Jermaine said, grabbing Lauren's hand. "Later, y'all."

Neither Lauren nor Jermaine said a word until they got inside the theater doors, and even then the conversation was strained at best. "Popcorn?" he asked.

"Sure."

"Soda?" he said, pulling what appeared to be a wad of crisp twenty-dollar bills out of his pocket.

"I'll take a bottled water — thanks," Lauren said, trying hard not to stare at the wad, lest Jermaine catch on that she was wondering just how a guy whose family was clearly low on cash came by that big of a money nut.

Frankly, Lauren didn't know what to say — what to think about this boy who'd hunted her down, invited her out, and made her feel all at once fascinated by and fearful of him, who seemed to be alternately impressed with and repulsed by her. So she just kept her mouth shut — a first for her.

"Oh, come on, that one's easy — Denzel!" Jermaine groaned at the movie screen, which was tossing up quizzes on movie stars. This question asked which African-American actor had won two Academy Awards.

Lauren looked at Jermaine, then back at the screen as she popped another piece of popcorn into her mouth. *He's one of the highest-grossing actors in history, but he's never cruised to the Oscars stage to pick up a statue. Who is he?*

"Oh, good grief," Lauren said, exasperated. "Tom Cruise. Who makes up these questions?"

"You're cute when you're agitated," Jermaine said, shifting his body to face Lauren's.

"Who said I was agitated?" Lauren said, popping another kernel into her mouth.

"Well, you didn't look too comfortable earlier."

Lauren took a swig of her bottled water, unsure what to say.

"Look, my bad for saying those things earlier. Can we forget all that happened and start over again?" Jermaine asked. He leaned into Lauren, turned her face toward his and planted a soft kiss on her lips. "Please?" he asked, going in for another kiss. "With sugar on top?" Another kiss.

Lauren looked into his eyes and melted all over again. Despite that her mind was crowded with all sorts of random thoughts about who this boy might be — gang member, drug dealer, welfare statistic, general all-around thug — her heart was speaking a whole different language. And when he leaned in for another kiss, this time, Lauren leaned in, too, parting her lips slightly to take in his tongue.

The lights dimmed, and the movie began.

11
SYDNEY

"Carmen. Rhea. For the last time, I'm just fine. There's nothing going on that I need or want to discuss," Sydney snapped irritably as the pounding in her temples threatened to reach a crescendo of epic proportions. She gingerly lifted her head off the ruffled pillow duster to look at the iHome clock on her bed stand. "Now, let me go. It's already seven-thirty at night, and I haven't even started to review those trig equations, let alone prepare for the weekly committee update I owe Principal Trumbull first thing in the morning. I'll see you guys tomorrow." And without waiting for a response from either of the two, Sydney hung up her phone.

Blessed silence immediately surrounded Sydney like the summer-weight down comforter she'd been camped out underneath since she arrived home from two hours of an after-school chemistry tutorial. For the past couple of days her phone had been ringing nonstop. If it wasn't her best friends trying to stage an A&E-worthy intervention for what they'd wrongly diagnosed as an SAT stress-induced meltdown, then it was Marcus repeatedly calling on the super damage-control mission for the "lack of attention" he'd been showing her lately. Funny how a little jealousy could get a brother back on track.

The scene in the cafeteria played itself over and over in Sydney's mind. Even though she could no longer recall everything word for word, the intensity of her anger when she spied Dara's hand lazily touching Marcus's knee under the table still made the hairs on her neck stand at attention. Not to mention the astonished looks on the faces of everyone within earshot of her final comment as she walked out. It was painfully obvious that her outburst on Tuesday had exposed everyone to a new side of Sydney. Granted, she may have been completely justified on every count of her behavior, from the elbow jab to the slick final comment, but at the end of the day, this was not a good look for the girl who had built her rep on maintaining perfect poise under pressure.

To make matters worse, despite the flowers, phone calls, and little love notes he left in her locker, something still didn't sit right with Sydney about Marcus's relationship with Dara. Which further complicated what was supposed to be a very discreet reconciliation process. Instead of spending quality time together, reestablishing their bonds of trust, she found herself ducking him at all costs. Which led to more questions from Carmen and Rhea. Like the small thread in that favorite hand-knitted cashmere scarf, one good yank and the entire thing just falls apart.

"Oww," Sydney whimpered as she gently dragged herself up and pushed the covers back. Using a technique she had learned from Jean-Claude during her last Reiki session, Sydney slowly massaged each temple to relieve some of the pressure as she walked across her bedroom into the adjacent bathroom. Working only with the dim light from the star-shaped nightlight, Sydney searched her medicine cabinet for any type of pain-relief medication. Finally locating the bottle of Aleve, she closed the medicine cabinet. Sydney paused for a moment to take in her reflection in the mirror. "It's fine. Everything is going to be fine . . . even Jackie O had to deal with Marilyn. You're Sydney Duke and you were built for this." The words of her little pep talk rang hollow in her own ear. Sighing, she opened the bottle and quickly popped two pills into her mouth. A gulp of tap water and Sydney turned back toward the beckoning bed. Just as she eased back into the warm spot under the covers, the sound of the front door being slammed closed echoed through the entire house.

"Can you believe that mess JV wants to call a routine?" Sydney couldn't help but hear Lauren screech incredulously. Her question was promptly followed by the sound of high-pitched laughter that could only belong to one person — Dara. Sydney grabbed one of her extra pillows and slammed it over her head to try to block the noise from below.

"I mean, seriously . . . And not for nothing: Is Jazmin putting on weight? 'Cause your girl ain't been hitting her herky jumps at all! And those knees are looking a little Beyoncé big, if you know what I'm saying?" Lauren proclaimed to the obvious enjoyment of Dara, whose laughter became increasingly shriller by the second.

"Ohmigod, I was thinking the same thing!" Dara half shouted between the laughter as the two moved through the house.

"I swear to God, those greedy little JV tramps must be stealing all of Varsity's snacks. It's like I can't win. The squads are like Nicole Richie before and after," Lauren continued just as loudly.

Unable to stand the grating sound of their voices a moment longer, Sydney sat straight up in the bed. "To hell with this," she muttered angrily as she slipped her feet into the pair of purple fuzzy slippers Marcus had given her when she caught the flu last year, and stood up. This was her friggin' house and Dara might be screwing her over elsewhere in the world, but not here.

Migraine forgotten, it took Sydney no time to get downstairs and into the den, where she found Lauren and Dara lounging comfortably in the stadium-sized seats watching a

TiVo'd episode of Tyra undercover as a homeless woman on the theater-sized big screen. As she stood in the doorway, looking at the back of both weaved heads, Sydney felt her blood pressure rapidly rise to the boiling point.

"Would you lower your voices, please?" Sydney commanded more than asked. Both girls did an about-face so fast, Sydney thought it a wonder that some of the tracks didn't come flying out.

"Excuse you?" Lauren asked angrily as Dara looked behind them to see if there might be someone else in the den who Sydney was addressing.

"You heard me," Sydney hissed, standing her ground. "I said: Lower. Your. Voices!"

"Okay, I don't know what the hell is wrong with you, but you need to stop. We're not even that loud," Lauren responded with a neck roll as she returned to watching Tyra and effectively ignored Sydney's request.

"Yeah, you are. And I'm trying to sleep upstairs," Sydney retorted.

"No, you ain't. Shoot, it's barely seven-thirty. What you're doing is being a miserable bitch. And I don't have the patience for it right now. So why don't you go 'head and get outta here," Lauren stated dismissively and turned up the volume.

"No, Lauren. Actually why don't you and your girl get

the hell up outta here!" Sydney screamed out hysterically, finally losing her cool.

"What'd you just say?" Lauren asked as she turned off the show completely and stood up to face her sister.

"I said turn down the volume or take your girl and go!" Sydney yelled again, this time looking dead at Dara as she stepped into the den. Lauren paused. She rarely saw her sister this angry, let alone at a friend of the family. She glanced over at Dara, who was clumsily rising to her feet.

"Sydney, I don't know what I have to do with . . ." Dara began, trying to steady the stammer in her voice.

"Oh, is that so?" Sydney was incredulous. She advanced menacingly on Dara, who was trying her best to get from between the row of seats before Sydney cornered her. "Well then, Dara, maybe you can tell me . . ." Sydney hesitated as she saw a familiar look of a deer caught in headlights pass over Dara's face. She realized that if she actually asked, there'd be no turning back.

"You need to stop screaming on my girl like that!" Lauren interjected, suddenly stepping forward to place herself between Dara and Sydney.

"Actually, all y'all need to stop this damn screaming in *my* goddamn house," thundered Altimus, suddenly appearing in the doorway to the surprise of all three girls. "I'm on the phone trying to conduct business and I can't even hear myself think. So I don't know what the hell is going on, but each of you has me very confused if you think any cussing and fighting is about to pop off up in here!"

Shocked back to her sensibilities, Sydney immediately turned back to face her furious stepfather. "I'm sorry. I didn't know you were home . . ."

"Clearly," he glowered.

"I was just trying to take a nap. They're too loud and I have a headache," Sydney continued now, holding her head for emphasis. She sincerely hoped he'd buy the "poor little sick girl" role because Altimus looked more than ready to put everyone in the room on an indefinite punishment.

"Altimus, she's bugging," Lauren countered. "We were minding our business, watching Tyra, and here she go talking about Dara has to leave!"

"Is that so? 'Cause last time I checked, I was the only one who has the right to throw folks out of this house." Altimus cocked his head to the side as he stared at the now much-subdued Sydney.

Sydney cleared her throat, "Yes, sir."

"That's what I thought. Now, tell you what. Lauren and Dara turn down the television and keep the noise to a minimum. Ain't no need to be screaming and carrying on like that unless you're working some corner. And, Sydney, you take your smart behind back to your room."

"But, but . . . I didn't do anything," she complained.

"Sydney Duke, I do not need the back talk. I said what I have to say, and you're keeping me from my money. Now go!"

"Fine," Sydney huffed as she stormed out of the room. She cut her eyes as she noticed Lauren triumphantly turning Tyra back on.

Sydney paced the length of her room in frustration. The last thing she expected was Altimus to pop up like that. As a general rule, he never conducted dealership business from the house because he said he wanted his house to feel like a home, not a satellite office. She didn't know if she was more upset about Altimus sending her to her room like a little kid or because her pride wouldn't allow her to ask Dara exactly what was going on with Marcus. She'd had the perfect opportunity right before bigmouth Lauren jumped in, but she just couldn't bring herself to say the words. But Dara's look spoke a thousand words. And, while a guilty facial appearance didn't constitute grounds for a breakup, she'd most definitely have to teach Marcus a lesson.

Of course, there was no way she was willing to come off like the woman scorned. That was so played out . . . and public. Carmen, Rhea, and anyone who knew her would lose all respect. Even in her worst moments, there was a limit to the stupidity.

Honestly, the Marcus solution was easy enough — now that she'd already planted the seeds of doubt in his head about the nature of her friendship with Jason (talk about perfect timing), she'd just continue to cozy up to the star football player. Maybe even attend a football game or two just to drive home the point. No need to come off as sluttish or cross any actual lines, just enough to show Marcus that if he didn't remember where his bread was buttered, there were others happy to eat.

And even though Sydney knew that Marcus was the only person she should be holding responsible for respecting their relationship, neither Dara nor Lauren were about to receive a get-out-of-jail-free card. Those two simply required more thought. They were so self-consumed, it was going to take a sledgehammer to make a dent. It's not like Sydney had anything that either wanted; in fact nobody did. The only thing Lauren or Dara cared two cents about was their untouchable image.

The sound of her phone beeping interrupted Sydney's thoughts. This time it was an e-mail blast from YRT notifying her that the latest posting was online.

As she reached for the button to silence the cell, it hit her. What better way to get back at Lauren and her snaggle-toothed sidekick than dropping a juicy little tidbit on YRT? How would little Ms. Dance Squad feel if the entire county knew that in her free time, Lauren continuously auditioned for low-budget uncut videos? And even worse, obviously didn't make the cut 'cause she ain't ever mentioned it? What about Dara? Wouldn't she love the world to know that she convinced her mother to use the child-support payments to pay for her to get a boob job? Granted, the boob job was actually a reduction for medical reasons, but still . . . didn't Lauren literally have to beg Altimus to pay for half of Dara's tuition last year because of it? Otherwise her ass would have straight been attending a public high school somewhere!

The more she thought about it, the more convinced Sydney became that this was the best way to handle it. After all, it was just a gossip site. Nobody actually *believed* the stories they read on it anyway. It's not like they couldn't deny if anyone asked — not that they would. It was Lauren and Dara. Not a soul at Brookhaven would dare question them directly — but they'd sure talk trash behind their backs. And even better, no one would ever figure out that it was actually her posting the info . . . except maybe for Lauren and Dara. And they'd damn sure never tell anyone, because that would require the both of them to admit the facts were true. Lauren and Dara would just have to suck it up and be a little uncomfortable in their skin for a couple of days. In the meantime, Sydney would emerge from the drama unscathed, looking like the decent, progressive, upstanding, and totally together individual she was, despite her trashy sister. It was perfect. Those hags would get a taste of their own medicine. As she sat down at her desk and eagerly logged on, a single smug thought worked its way through Sydney's head: "I can't wait to see just how far away from Dara Marcus wants to move now!"

12
LAUREN

"Aw hell, no!" Lauren screamed as she punched the stop button on the dance team's portable CD player and jumped off the bleachers. "What are y'all doing? You're moving your feet like you got hot crap in your Reeboks."

Dara shook her head and smirked at the seven uniform-clad squad members as Lauren took her place in front of them, her ponytail swinging with every angry step. They'd put the finishing touches on the new Homecoming routine the night before, and had every intention of perfecting it at Lauren's house after watching Tyra, but Sydney's ridiculous outburst put a premature end to that. Lauren was a little nervous about it: The Homecoming performance would be her first as the dance-squad captain and she needed it to be tight because, well, she had a rep to protect, and the last thing she wanted to do was get out in front of all of Brookhaven Prep students, alumni, and her former dance-squad-captain's mom looking like a straight amateur. Still, Lauren was confident that the number she created was hot, and she and Dara had nailed it enough to show it to the squad and work out the kinks during rehearsals.

"Somebody please explain to me why half of you are stepping out to the right on three when I clearly said hit left on three, then step, pop, pop, and turn," Lauren said angrily, doing the steps for emphasis. "I mean, somebody help me out here, 'cause if it's too damn confusing, then maybe I can go get somebody who can get it right. There's some seventh graders on JV looking for a shot."

No one on the team said anything, though a few folded their arms and twisted their lips in a "yeah, whatever" kind of way, and one, LaTanya, snickered.

"Oh, what? I'm funny now? I'm Chris Rock up in here?" Lauren said, getting into LaTanya's face. She was seeing red — and about mad enough to pop a vein.

LaTanya shifted her feet and folded her arms, staring right back into Lauren's eyes. She didn't say a word — didn't have to; her eyes did the talking. Lauren was taken aback.

"Did I stutter, LaTanya? I said, 'Do you think I'm funny?'"

LaTanya looked at a couple of the dance-squad members

standing closest to her, then back at Lauren, and smirked but said nothing.

Thought not. Lauren took her place in front of the squad, her back to the girls. "Dara, hit play so I can show them how it's done — again," she said, standing in the starting position.

The intro bass to Ludacris's "MoneyMaker" thumped against the gym walls as Lauren snapped her fingers and bopped her knees to the beat. Like she did every time she performed, she focused her eyes on one person — today, it was Dara — as she prepared to execute her moves; doing so helped her concentrate and connect with the audience all at once, a trick her mother taught her from her dance-captain days. When Luda's voice slid through the speakers, Lauren took off — hip shake, double gyrate to the left, and then to the right, swizzle to the front, chest pop one, chest pop two, step left, step left, body roll, step, pop, pop . . . trip, slip, almost fall.

The horror in Dara's eyes mirrored those of Lauren, who instinctively hobbled to her right foot to take the pressure off her twisted left one. But it wasn't the slip up or even the pain that had Lauren reeling; it was the fact that the entire squad had burst into hysterics over Lauren's misstep.

Dara stopped the music and rushed over to help Lauren to the bleachers, getting there in time to hear LaTanya not-so-whisper, "Definitely wouldn't see that in a Thug Heaven video." Dara wasn't so sure what she meant at first, but Lauren's head shot up instantly. How did she know about the Thug Heaven thing? Did she know about it, for real? Ohmigod, maybe she was at the audition and saw? Or maybe she showed up in one of those blooper clips on that new BET show, *Not Never*, where they chronicle on-set mishaps of the most popular rap and R&B videos. Would it have been on that show that quickly? Nah, Lauren deduced just as quickly as she'd questioned; there was no way LaTanya or anyone else for that matter would know about the unfortunate video tryout — no way. But why was she referencing Thug Heaven?

"Whatever, young'uns — I look more graceful falling than you do executing my moves," Lauren said, trying to shake off the mishap and LaTanya's comment.

A couple of the girls play-coughed and giggled, like they were in on some kind of joke Lauren and Dara weren't privy to. Lauren tried her best to shake it off. "Dara, why don't you lead them through the steps so I can see who's throwing everybody off? Maybe she can put on the mascot uniform while the rest of us get it right for the Homecoming game," Lauren said icily, her words practically scrubbing the smiles off the team members' faces.

"No problem," Dara said just as seriously as she took her place in front of the group. They all fell into position behind her. "Let's do it without the music so we can count it off. Five, six, seven, eight!"

Dara was so busy counting and working her way through the dance routine that she didn't really see the three football players tumble into the gymnasium, snickering and gawking at the girls like they were about to pull some dollar bills out of their pockets. One, Brad Whitfield, started dancing like he could hear music; he made the number twelve on his chest bounce so hard it almost looked like he was shaking breasts.

"Um, excuse me, like the sign says on the door, this is a closed rehearsal — but obviously you would know that if you could read," Lauren practically shouted, as the dancing came to a halt.

"Oh, no, excuse me," Brad said, standing up straight as an arrow. "My bad, it does say this is a closed rehearsal. But make no question about it, a brother can read," he said, laughing and giving pounds to his boys, who were laughing, too.

Lauren, completely thrown by the behavior, wasn't quite sure what to make of the continued interruption — surely the football players knew that the dance squad's practices were as sacrosanct as their own football practices. What in the hell were they doing?

"I'm quite pleased that you can read, Brad — wouldn't want your scholarship to go to waste here at Brookhaven Prep," Lauren sneered. "Can you excuse us, please?"

Brad stopped laughing — that insult was going to bleed.

"Oh, well, you know, at least up in my house, the extra cash goes to the fundamentals," Brad answered back smoothly. "Maybe my parents could give your girl Dara and her moms some tips on how to spend more wisely." And then he bounced that number twelve some and gave his boys more pounds, their slaps and finger snaps punctuated by roaring laughter echoing off the gymnasium walls.

Lauren looked at Dara, who was staring at the boys and all the squad members, clearly confused. She gave a pleading look to Lauren, who returned the look with a "what the hell?" right back. Lauren watched as Brad and his friends tumbled back out of the gym, then turned her attention back to the squad. She stood up gingerly on the bleachers, folded her arms, and said in almost a whisper, "Shut the hell up."

The girls, still laughing, barely heard her.

She said it again, just as quietly.

Still laughter.

"I . . . said . . . shut . . . the . . . hell . . . up!" Lauren screamed loud enough to practically stop the rotation of nature — chirping birds, whistling winds, running stream water, all of that. "I don't know what's gotten into you all today, but I'll tell you this: Today's going to be the last day you waste my time with this bullshit. Check it: I want y'all to go home and think real hard about whether you want to be on this squad and the reasons why, because when tomorrow comes, anybody who isn't taking this seriously enough to get the steps right and treat me and my co-captain with the respect we deserve? Oh, trust: You won't get a gig dancing for your local kindergarten Easter assembly. Try my ass!" Lauren yelled as she snatched up her CD player and stepped gingerly off the bleachers. "Let's go, Dara. Later for them."

Dara looked unsurely at her teammates as she walked slowly toward the bleachers and grabbed her book bag. She could hear the girls whispering as she and Lauren made their way to the door, but this time she couldn't make out a word they were saying.

"What the hell was that all about?" Lauren demanded as the two girls pushed through the gymnasium door. The slamming door made Dara jump. "Seems like the whole world is tripping today. The girls are bugging out in practice, football players gone wild. Even Charlie the Boozer Loser rolled up on me today, breath smelling like White Lightning, talking about how I should let him take me out. Now that Negro knows good and well . . ."

"I haven't a clue what all of this is about, but you're not the only one feeling it," Dara said quietly. "I was going to tell you after practice that someone left a really screwy picture on my locker; there were two stick figures — one had pin points for breasts, and under it, it said 'before,' and then the other one had big circles for breasts, and under that one it said 'after.' I don't know what the hell it means, and I was thinking whoever drew it put it on the wrong locker. But now I'm starting to wonder . . ."

"Yeah, probably was the wrong locker," Lauren said as they walked toward her locker, hoping her words would soothe the worried look that had settled on her best friend's brow. "Or maybe ol' Miss Candy slipped something into the chocolate sludge she was passing off as pudding in the cafeteria today."

"Yeah, maybe," Dara said, obviously still worried. "You going to the Homecoming decorations committee meeting?"

"Nah — I don't feel like it."

Dara was quiet — too quiet.

Lauren dialed the combination on her locker, snatched open the door, dropped her Social Studies book into the bottom of the slim cubicle, and grabbed her jacket. By the time she finally assembled her things and slammed the locker shut, Dara was slumped against the neighboring locker, staring at her sneakers. "Look," Lauren said, turning to face her friend. "I want to apologize to you for what happened last night with Syd — she's buggin' out because of Altimus tripping with my car and making her share, and she's probably feeling the pressure of being Little Miss Perfect for her Benefit Gala debacle coming up. She's definitely coming undone. But it's really got nothing to do with you." Lauren looked around the hallway to make sure no one was listening in. "Besides, you and ol' boy are no more, so it can't be about that, right?"

More silence from Dara.

"Right?" Lauren said, a little more forcefully.

"Right," Dara said weakly.

"Then cool," Lauren said, squaring her shoulders and heading for the exit, Dara following her. "Don't worry, be happy and shit."

Dara giggled, if only a little, as the two of them headed quietly toward the parking lot. Lauren ticked off a mental list of things she'd do when she got home: wash her face and moisturize, run the flat iron over her hair and wrap it, have Edwina make her a little snack, head up to her bed to watch *Girlfriends*, *I Love New York*, and whatever was on BET.

What the — ?

Sydney's car, which Lauren had driven to school, was not there. In the space reserved for the captain of the dance squad. Fourth to the left of the science building. Where she parked it that morning.

"Oh, shit, where's the car?" Lauren yelled as she and Dara came to a standstill. She spun around, her eyes searching frantically for the shiny silver Saab, a near twin to her own confiscated black one. There were only about seven cars in the lot — one of them Dara's red Audi.

"Are you sure you parked it here?"

"Dara, where else would I park the damn car? That's my space!"

"Okay, okay — calm down," Dara said, holding up her hands in defense. "Stop and think a minute. We had lunch together so you didn't drive it then."

"Dara, I know I parked it right here!"

"Okay, check your purse — you still have the keys? Maybe Sydney took the car?"

Lauren reached into her purse and pulled out the keys — she had them, so there was no way Sydney would have driven off in it, right? Keisha had laid down that law this morning when Lauren announced she'd be using the car because she had a late practice and a Homecoming decoration committee meeting. Sydney protested, tossing up that she had to go with the Benefit Gala committee to look at the ballroom they'd chosen, but, as Lauren pointed out, Marcus had a car, and since he was the "bestest boyfriend in the whole universe, he can just pick you up and bring you home."

"Lauren! That's my car! I decide when I drive it, and I decide when I want my boyfriend to take me somewhere — don't get it twisted."

"Ain't nobody up in here twisted but you," Lauren shouted back. "Run me the keys — I need to get home somehow."

"The Yellow Pages are in the drawer right over there — it's

got plenty of numbers for taxicab services. I suggest you get real familiar with them."

"Oh, stop it — the both of you," Keisha interrupted, sauntering into the kitchen, her silky cream bathrobe and gown flowing behind her. "Sydney, just call Marcus; I'm sure he'll be glad to give you a ride. And you, young lady," Keisha said, turning to Lauren, "make sure you get her car back here in one piece. You all didn't finish up the bacon, did you?"

No — Sydney wouldn't have defied their mother and taken the car, Lauren quickly deduced. And besides, Marcus's car wasn't in the lot, either. "No, Sydney does not have the car — I know she doesn't," Lauren said to Dara.

Which meant only one thing: The car had been stolen.

"Ohmigod," Lauren shouted over and over as she broke into a fast trot back toward the main office, Dara in tow. She fully intended to tell Ms. Campbell, the front office coordinator, to dial 911 and report the car stolen. As she ran, she pulled her Sidekick out of her purse and pushed frantically through her list of contacts to find Altimus's private cell phone number. Her heart was pounding hard enough to be seen practically through her baby-blue dance-squad velour sweatsuit.

Just as she found Altimus's number and her fingers touched the door to the school, her Sidekick rang in her hands — startling her just a bit. It was Sydney.

"Stop running through the parking lot like somebody stole something from you — I have the car," Sydney said. Just then, a car horn sounded; instinctively, Lauren looked up. It was Sydney, speeding by the front of Brookhaven Prep, waving like she didn't have a lick of sense. "You might want to ask Dara if she can give you a ride — I got things to do with *my car*."

And with that, Sydney hung up.

"Wasn't that Sydney in the silver Saab?" Dara asked, looking confused and pointing at the car speeding through the stop sign and out onto the street.

"Shit!" Lauren yelled, slamming her phone shut. Before it could even click closed, it sounded again — this time, a text message from Donald. The subject line said "READ THIS NOW!"

Still huffing, Lauren scrolled down and read the message:

U R not going to believe this. I got FW from a friend at yr skul. So did the rest of yr skul. 3 guess who knows all this abt U? And which foot R U gonna put in her ass? D.

Lauren scrolled down some more; with each word she took in, her mouth opened wider.

"What's wrong?" Dara said, alarmed by the look on Lauren's face.

Lauren just kept cursing and scrolling, cursing and scrolling some more. And then, finally, she handed her Sidekick over to Dara. And now, it was her time to curse.

She may be Brookhaven Prep's most famous dancer, but LD's moves meant nothing on the set of Thug Heaven's "Still Ghetto," where, even after giving Dough Boy a little taste of her Laffy Taffy, she couldn't shake her way into the video.

But at least what she's shaking is real . . . can't say the same for BP's other dancing queen, DS, who can shake not only what her mama gave her, but what her money-maker daddy paid for too. Glad to see those support checks put to good use at the offices of Dr. "Make me look like Pam Lee."

What a pair.

"Oh, my God, who did you tell about my breast operation?" Dara yelled, tears welling in her eyes. "I can't believe you . . ."

"Wait a minute, Dara, I'm not the one you should be getting mad at — I didn't send this to the whole world."

"Then who did? I mean, the only way anyone could have known about it was if you told, seeing as only you and my mother know about it. The person I trusted the most in this whole world told my most intimate secrets. I can't believe this," Dara said, handing Lauren's phone back to her. "I trusted you."

"Oh, come on, now — you're no angel, either," Lauren shot back, snatching her phone from Dara's hand. "You're directing your anger to the wrong person. And besides, you're not the only one screwed here — the whole school thinks I'm a whore who gave it up to some dirty-ass rapper."

"Well if the shoe fits . . ." Dara said, scratching her hair and rolling her eyes.

"I know you're not even taking it there. Ain't nobody over in this direction a tramp," Lauren shouted. "Besides, you got some nerve, considering your tongue was all down my sister's boyfriend's throat!"

"Oh, you know what? I don't need this!" Dara said, stomping off toward her car.

"Whatever . . ." Lauren said, pushing her Sidekick into her purse and grabbing her car keys as she stomped off into the direction of her parking space.

And then she remembered — she had no way home.

13
SYDNEY

"Ring the alarm! I been through this too long, but I'll be damned if I see another chick on your arm . . ." screeched Beyoncé from the iPod dock as Sydney stood in the middle of her walk-in closet, nodding along in full agreement. "Mmm-hmm, tell it girl," she muttered to no one in particular as she punched in the numbers to her Aunt Lorraine's house and pulled out one of the many dresser drawers in search of a top to wear to dinner that night. "Aha! I knew it was in here some-where," she exclaimed victoriously, pulling her white Malandrino wrap top with the detailed navy cuffs out from underneath a pile of camis and T-shirts as the phone started to ring. Putting it on over the gray lace tank she was already wearing, Sydney turned to inspect herself from every angle in one of the closet's full-length mirrors. "I guess . . ." she said, approving her outfit to herself.

"Hello?"

"Hey, Dad, it's me," she answered as a huge grin spread across her face.

"Oh, hey, Ladybug, what's going on," he replied with a slight cough.

"I'm just calling to see how you're feeling, is all," she continued as she started to play with her hair.

"Oh, I'm so much better today. It's hard being home and not being able to go nowhere 'cause I haven't found work yet. You know I'm not the type of man who can sit around too long. These streets stay calling my name. Soon, I'm just gonna have to make something happen. . . ."

"Don't get frustrated, Dad," Sydney encouraged. "Something will open up. I can feel it."

"I know, I know," he muttered.

"To be perfectly honest, I haven't been feeling so great myself lately. But I'm working it out."

"What's going on with you, Syd? Everything okay at home? Your mother don't know . . ."

"No, nothing like that. Mom doesn't have the slightest clue. It's just —" A persistent knock at her bedroom door interrupted her midsentence. "Hey, Dad, someone's at my door; I gotta go," she said hurriedly in a much lower voice.

"Okay, sweetie, I'll talk to you soon."

"Love you," Sydney barely squeezed out before ending the call. "Come in," she instructed as she turned off the light and headed toward the slowly opening door.

"Sorry to bother you, Ms. Sydney," started Edwina before she even opened the door completely, "but Marcus is here."

A quick glance at her Tag showed Sydney that it was only 5:40 P.M. Dammit, he was early. That used to be one of the things she loved about Marcus. Now it just translated into five extra minutes that she would have to spend with him . . . and one less she got to spend talking to her dad. "Is he in the den?" Sydney questioned with a sigh.

"Yes, miss. Do you want me to tell him that you'll be down shortly?" Edwina offered helpfully.

Sydney paused as she seriously considered letting Marcus sit and stew. As much as she enjoyed the idea, Sydney knew that they needed to break the growing ice between them before it got out of hand or, even worse, got back to her parents. Truth be told, it would take Keisha less than thirty seconds flat to sniff out a problem between the once symbiotic couple. Lord knows Sydney did not want her relationship issues to become the main topic of discussion at the dinner table . . . especially with Lauren and her fake-ass boyfriend, Donald, sitting there like vultures waiting for the fresh kill. "Actually, can you escort him upstairs?"

135

"Yes, of course. I'll be right back," Edwina replied with a nod and softly closed the door behind her.

Sydney turned back to her desk and lowered the volume on her iPod dock. As much as she fought the feeling, she missed Marcus. Not for nothing, being bitchy all the time was freaking exhausting. It seemed unfathomable for Dice to be home for almost two weeks and yet she hadn't so much as mentioned it to Marcus. A soft knock announced his arrival. "Oh, well," she muttered before opening the door.

"Hey," Marcus said gently in greeting.

"Come in," Sydney replied, stepping back to allow him to enter. "Have a seat. I'm pretty much dressed . . ."

"Thanks. These are for you," he said, shyly offering Sydney a small bouquet of hot-pink Gerber daisies as he stepped in the room and headed over toward the bed. "You look really nice. Isn't that the top Carmen bought you for your birthday last year?"

"Thanks. It is," Sydney replied softly, already feeling her resolve getting weak. Marcus was always so good with the details. "I haven't had a chance to wear it as much as I probably should, but you know how that goes." She shut the door and turned to look at Marcus. He was wearing the navy-and-green argyle Ralph Lauren sweater and dark blue Rock & Republic denim outfit she bought him at the start of the school year. Lord, he looked good.

"I hear ya . . ." Marcus trailed off as he sat down on her

bed and looked around the room slowly. "Wasn't sure I'd ever see this place again," he said with a slight smile.

"Yeah, well, neither was I," Sydney countered as she walked over and sat beside him. She inspected the bouquet thoughtfully while Marcus played with the end of a stray dreadlock. An uncomfortable silence stretched between them.

"You know, I really am sorry about not telling you about Dara," Marcus offered. "Seriously, I had no idea that hanging out with other girls would bother you so much."

"It doesn't bother me that you're hanging out with another girl." Sydney measured her words carefully. She definitely didn't want to get into a debate with him right before they sat down to dinner. "It's the fact that you hid it from me."

"I did not hide it from you," Marcus asserted. "I simply did not bring it up."

Sydney instantly scooted away at the first sign of Marcus's righteous ego rearing its ugly head. "That's funny, *babe*, 'cause somehow you manage to bring up everything else under the sun, like: how long it takes me to answer the phone when you call, or where I'm going with my girls, and, oh, how could I forget, how do I know Jason Danden? You damn sure didn't forget to bring that one up, Marcus!"

"Sydney, please, it's hardly the same thing. Dara is your sister's best friend. Jason is some richie jock who moved here from New York City. There's no reason for you to be associating that closely with him," Marcus retaliated defensively.

"I'm curious — since when were you supposed to be the one telling me who I need and don't need to know?"

"Okay, okay, you're right. I'm sorry." Marcus threw his hands up in mock defeat. "I should've told you about Dara."

Sydney stared at Marcus suspiciously. That apology came a little too quickly for her liking. She knew Marcus and how much he hated having to apologize for anything. "It's not just that . . . ."

"And, yes, I definitely shouldn't have told you that I don't have to tell you about all my friends. I was out of line," Marcus continued as he closed the distance between them on the bed. "But will you please, please, please, stop being mad at me now? 'Cause I'm not feeling this tension between us. I miss my li'l Syd-Bear," he mumbled gently into her ear. Sydney half heartedly tried to pull away but the tingly sensations running up and down her neck were too much. He was always *so damn good* with the details.

Sydney slowly inhaled and exhaled before she stood up and started straightening herself out. "We should head down; I'm pretty sure it's almost six o'clock by now."

Marcus reached out and grabbed Sydney around the waist. "So we're cool?"

Sydney just smiled and pulled him up to join her. She had no intention of letting Marcus off the hook, but he didn't need to know all that just yet. "Yeah, yeah, yeah, let's go down before my mom catches a fit. You know how she gets about these ridiculous family sit-downs."

"Anything you say, my dear," Marcus agreed with a playful squeeze of her butt. "Damn, I missed that," he said as he opened her door and waited for Sydney to pass by.

"I'm so sure," Sydney replied as she walked out and they headed downstairs.

As soon as the two entered the Dukes' massive dining room area, Lauren started in on Sydney. "Well, isn't it so nice of Bob Marley and Sista Souljah to join us for dinner?" she questioned sarcastically while Donald barely suppressed a giggle with a fake cough.

Sydney wordlessly sucked her teeth in response. She knew Lauren was fixing for a fight with her ever since she'd left that ass stranded in the middle of the Brookhaven parking lot after cheerleading practice. Little did Ms. Thang know, that stunt was just the beginning if she didn't back off.

"Lauren, that's enough. Marcus and Sydney, please have a seat," Altimus gestured at the two empty chairs across the table from Lauren and Donald.

"I apologize for keeping Syd," Marcus offered as he pulled out Sydney's seat for her. "I wanted to review some stuff about the next community project I asked Sydney to help me chair. The time just slipped by . . ." Sydney listened quietly at the ease of Marcus's lie as she scooted in.

"Well, anything that's going to put my baby one step closer to a Brown acceptance letter is worth a five-minute wait," Altimus offered with an approving nod.

"Absolutely," agreed Mrs. Duke.

"Oh, and before I forget to tell you, my mom sends her best," he offered with the smile Sydney found so difficult to resist.

"How nice of her; be sure to return the greetings." Keisha grinned broadly. "I certainly hope that we'll be seeing the Councilwoman at the anniversary party."

"I'm sure she'll do her best, ma'am," Marcus replied. He seemed to be laying it on extra thick with her parents. Sydney briefly wondered if her friends ever felt he did the same thing when dealing with her.

As soon as Edwina finished pouring Sydney and Marcus their glasses of water, Mrs. Duke set in. "Before Altimus says grace, I just want to thank you boys for coming to dinner tonight," she said, addressing Donald and Marcus. "With only a few weeks left until my party —"

"Ahem," Altimus cleared his throat. "Don't you mean *our* party, Keish?"

"Yes, yes, *our* party," she corrected herself with a playful roll of the eyes. "Like I was saying, with only a few weeks left, there are logistics and responsibilities that I need to go over. As I'm sure you can understand, it's extremely important that the twins' escorts make them look as good as possible at all times."

"Now, Mrs. Duke, you know I loves to make my Lauren look good," Donald interjected a little too brightly as he planted an unexpected and noticeably moist kiss on Lauren's left cheek. Sydney recoiled at Donald's overzealous gesture.

"That's so gross," Syd mumbled not so discreetly. Under the table, Marcus put a restraining hand on Sydney's knee. Lauren turned to look at her sharply.

"Is there a problem, Sydney?" Altimus inquired from his end of the table.

"No, sir, there's no problem," Sydney responded and then turned to face her mom. "Mother, I'm quite sure Marcus doesn't need to be brought up to speed on how to behave at your party. Some of us already understand appropriate social etiquette." She finished by staring down Donald.

"Yeah, yeah, can we eat before I, oh, I don't know, throw up in my mouth?" Lauren blurted out to the appalled response of everyone at the dinner table.

"What in the world?" Mrs. Duke gasped, mouth agape.

"Eww, you hateful bitch!" Sydney spat.

"Lauren! Sydney! I don't know what has gotten into you two this evening but I have had just about enough!" Altimus barked. "You both need to apologize to this entire table immediately!"

"I'm sorry," Sydney said, immediately apologizing.

"Whatever," Lauren continued defiantly. "I can't help being honest."

"That's it, young lady." Keisha jumped up from her seat and pointed at the door. "Carry your little ass upstairs. If you don't know how to act, then don't nobody need to be around you!"

"Fine. Feel free to punish me for speaking the truth when Little Miss Perfect sits there hiding things right in front of your faces," Lauren snapped as she slowly stood up to leave the table.

"Excuse you?" Sydney countered once again, looking directly at Donald, wearing his pink polka-dot Versace fitted shirt. "How am *I* the one hiding things?"

"Sydney, don't even get involved," Marcus whispered beneath his breath.

Lauren paused dramatically as if preparing for the kill. "Oh, no? So you weren't the one running over to Aunt Lorraine's house to go see Dice last week?" Not finished yet, Lauren whipped out her cell phone, and with the press of a button played on the speakerphone a recent message from their dad begging Lauren to come with her sister the next time Sydney stopped by. The room went silent enough to hear a pin drop.

"What the hell?" Keisha roared at Sydney. "Did I not tell you that I didn't want you speaking to that man? Did I not?

Seventeen years, you ungrateful little heiffa! I take care of you, I put clothes on your back, and this is what I get in return? Your ass to kiss? That low-budget gun-smuggling convict never did a damn thing for you, and you go behind my back and side with him?"

"Mom, he's my . . ." Sydney began as the hot tears started rolling. Lauren stood smiling smugly at the door.

"He's not *shit*. You hear me? The man that put a roof over your head for the past twelve years is the only father you have! And I'll be damned — "

"He's not some monster," Sydney exclaimed, jumping to her feet. "You just want me to be as evil and coldhearted as you are, but I won't! He loves me!"

"Do not say another word," hissed Altimus as he slowly stood. "Not another word. You will not disrespect your mother or this house. I don't care what you think or what ridiculous lies that man has filled your head with, but *your mother* told you not to have anything to do with him. And as long as you live here, what *we* say goes. From this moment on, consider yourself on indefinite punishment. No more phone, no more car, no more weekend anything! It's over. Until further notice, I'll be hiring a driver to take and pick you up from everywhere you need to go."

"Oh, snap," Donald said as his eyes widened in glee at the Duke family carnage.

Consumed with rage and embarrassment at being

caught out, Sydney stormed toward the door past Lauren. She stopped just outside of the doorway and then turned around to face the room with her final thought: "You shut your closeted ass up, Donald! You don't get to say shit about me until you figure out how to tell your parents that you like boys!"

14
LAUREN

It was still fall, but the crisp, chilled Atlanta air smelled like winter — like burning oak and cedar and pine. Smoky. Lauren loved the scent; it reminded her of when she was a little girl and Altimus would take her and Sydney into his library and light a fire in the mammoth brick-and-granite structure and let the girls curl up in his huge leather chairs. If Sydney got her way, he'd read book after book after book. But on the days Lauren had his ear, Altimus would let her talk him into taking them out into their expansive backyard to count the stars peeking through the trees. They looked the best on nights like this, when the colorful leaves dropped like rain on manicured lawns, creating wide gaps of midnight-blue sky between the branches. That's when folks turned to their fireplaces for that warmth, that comfort — that Atlanta winter smell.

But tonight, not even her favorite scent could make Lauren feel comfortable. The mess with Sydney, the dinner blowup, the e-mail about her and Dara — all of that had Lauren off-kilter, and there was only one person she could think of to set her right, only one person who wasn't in the middle of all the drama: Jermaine. And she wanted that consolation in person, because on this particular night, the cell phone wasn't enough.

"But how you gonna get here?" he'd asked earlier, when Lauren called him to inform him of her big Buckhead escape.

"I don't know — I'll take a cab," she said quickly, mentally kicking herself in the ass for not thinking of grabbing a few cab numbers before she snuck out the sunroom window, the only first-floor exit that didn't have an alarm sensor. She was already trudging through the leaves in the neighbor's yard, presumably safe from the prying eyes of Keisha's security cameras.

"That's gonna cost you like at least fifty or sixty dollars. You can't waste that kind of money," he said.

"Don't they take debit cards?" Lauren asked as she finally made it to the sidewalk.

Jermaine chuckled. "Babe, taxicabs don't take debit cards. Cash-only business."

"Damn," Lauren said, taking a mental snapshot of the cash contents of her wallet. There might have been about eleven dollars in there. Maybe. "Then come get me. I can meet you on Ponce. I can walk there and — "

"Whoa, whoa. It's close to eleven at night. You can't be walking around like that by yourself."

"Jermaine. I live in Buckhead. Nobody's outside, and no one is going to do anything to me. Now, are you going to come get me or what?"

"Babe, I can't. I don't have my car." His brother had his car. Again. "I know — get on the MARTA train. I can meet you at the West End Station."

Lauren really didn't want to tell Jermaine that though she'd lived in Atlanta all her life, she'd been on MARTA only once — the day Altimus dragged her and Sydney, then about thirteen years old, to an Atlanta Falcons game. None of the Duke women could figure out, even years later, what was going through his mind when he decided his quality Daddy-and-the-twins time should be spent in a massive stadium full of drunken, foul-mouthed, rowdy football fans. But some-how, Altimus thought it was a great way to bond with his girls and give them, as he put it, "a new experience." It was an experience, all right — a horrifying one that began with oodles of Falcons fans tumbling onto their train, already half-drunk and calling out their "who-hoos" and tossing high fives and trading football stories and stats like they were paid Super Bowl commentators, and ended with Altimus cursing out some big, fat, sweaty white guy (dripping in red and black,

147

literally, from his spray-painted hair to his old-school Converse) for pushing up too close to Lauren and Sydney as the entire trainful of passengers transferred onto another dingy train on the West Line. "You best watch where you puttin' your hands," Altimus said with a tone neither of the girls had ever heard him use before. His eyes were narrowed like slits; his spine was so straight that, even though the sweaty guy was about his same height, Altimus seemed to tower over him. Lauren almost felt sorry for the guy. Almost.

"Sorry, bro . . ." the guy began.

"I ain't your bro," Altimus shot back. "Back off my girls."

Lauren decided that day that nothing on God's green earth could convince her she'd ever set foot on somebody's MARTA train. But then again, she never imagined she'd have a reason to be in the West End, either. But this night, she wanted — needed — to be there. And seeing as her car was off-limits — Sydney's keys had been confiscated from both girls — and there was no way in hell she was going to call in a favor with Dara, who still wasn't really talking to her, MARTA it would be.

"You're going to meet me, right?" Lauren said nervously.

"Yeah," Jermaine said. "Just get on the North–South line, headed south. I'll be standing at the exit."

Within fifteen minutes, Lauren was sitting on a train, squeezed up against the cold window, hoping the cooties of the thousands of commoners who had ridden that nasty train throughout the day wouldn't rub off on her. There were only a few people riding with her — a girl about her age, sitting with some boy who looked like he was straight off the set of *Menace II Society*; an older woman in a uniform, maybe a waitress or office cleaner; two men in work suits; and the thirty-something guy in a dirty, dusty, funky coat sitting closest to her. He stank. Lauren, horrified at the prospect of having to smell him much longer, pulled a tissue from her purse and not so discreetly held it over her nose until the computerized voice on the loudspeaker said, "Next stop, West End."

And when she stepped out of the door and ran up the stairs and toward the exit, there he was. The tears welled in her eyes with each step and turned into a full-on sloppy cry when she fell into his arms.

"Damn, babe," he said, squeezing her in his embrace. "It's going to be all right. Come on, don't cry."

"It's all just a shitty mess, and I don't know how to fix it, Jermaine," Lauren sobbed. "I can't take this — I just can't."

"I know, I know — shh. It's going to be all right," he said. Jermaine pushed Lauren back, tilted her head up toward his, and kissed her lips. "Come on, let's get outta here. My man let me borrow his car; it's parked right up the steps," he said, wiping the tears from her eyes and grabbing her hand. They walked out into the bright streetlights of the still bustling neighborhood.

Lauren didn't know what to expect or how to act walking into the tiny, decrepit house Jermaine called home. After all, what do you say to someone whose place could practically fit into your foyer: Love what you've done with the place? Nice "vintage" furniture? I'm feeling that old, stale-fish smell, reminds me of home?

Jermaine sensed her discomfort. "Well it ain't much, I know, but it's home," he mumbled, looking around at his place almost as if it were the first time he'd seen it, too.

Lauren wiped her eyes some more and folded her arms. She heard some movement in a room toward the back of the house. "Your mom here?" she asked, startled.

"Nah, she's, um, out," Jermaine said. "That's my brother."

"I didn't know you had a brother," Lauren said.

"Yeah, well, I do. He ain't around here much."

"Oh," Lauren said, growing uncomfortable. She was so sure that running to Jermaine was the right thing to do, but just then she started to question what the hell she was going through when she decided it was a good idea to darken a doorway in the West End after midnight. "You know, maybe I should go," she said.

"No," Jermaine said softly, taking her hands into his. "No, stay. I'll drive you home in a little while. Just — just stay. Let me talk to you. I want to know what happened."

He led her to his room, which was down a small hallway just off the living room/dining room area. It was neat — a small bed covered with a hand-sewn quilt was pushed up against the white wall next to a small window overlooking the faded yellow siding of the neighbor's house. An iPod hooked up to a speaker sat on a small, rusted table next to the bed, squeezed next to a metal folding chair. Sneaker boxes were piled one on top of the other in the closet, which was covered awkwardly by a curtain that Jermaine hadn't gotten around to closing.

"Soooo . . . this is where the magic happens, huh?"

"Oh, you got jokes, huh, Ms. Duke?" Jermaine laughed.

"Actually, I'm not really in a joking kind of mood," Lauren said, getting quiet.

"Just trying to lighten the mood up a little, you know . . ." Jermaine said, extending his hand to invite her to sit on his bed.

Lauren gave a half smile and sat on the folding chair next to the table. Jermaine chuckled and fell backward onto his bed.

"So?"

"So?" Lauren mimicked back.

"What happened? Whose ass I got to kick tonight?"

Lauren looked down at her hands and fiddled with her fingernails, buying herself time while she decided just how much she wanted to tell this boy. She looked up and into his eyes and, without having one good reason why she should trust him, Lauren let the events of the past few weeks — the Dara and Marcus mess, the dance-squad debacle, the nasty e-mail, Sydney's outing Donald — tumble from her lips.

"I mean, everybody thinks that just because we're twins we're supposed to act alike, too, but my sister and I are two totally different people and there's no changing that," Lauren said, getting teary again. "We fight like everybody else, and every once in a while it gets a little nastier than it should, but what she did this time was bananas. What's worse is that I'm starting to think she had something to do with that e-mail."

"But why would she tell everybody you was shaking your ass in a video? That's some foul stuff that nobody would even believe —" Jermaine began.

Lauren cut him off. "Well, uh, thing is . . ." she hesitated, trying to find the right words to explain why she was at the video shoot in the first place.

Jermaine laughed. "Hold up — you did try out for a Thug Heaven video?"

"It's not funny, Jermaine," Lauren shot back, jumping out of her chair.

"No, no, come on, I'm not laughing at you," Jermaine said. "It's just that, you know, you all from Buckhead and whatnot, dressed in the hot clothes, riding in the hot car, Daddy all rich and stuff. I can't really picture you getting grimy on a Thug Heaven video set."

"I didn't get grimy, Jermaine!" Lauren sneered.

"I'm sorry, I didn't mean it that way . . ."

"Then what did you mean, Jermaine?" Lauren asked as she paced the room. "I mean, if I wanted to be judged I could have stayed home."

Jermaine stood up and pulled Lauren to him. "Come on, baby, I'm not judging you. I'm here for you — you know that," he said, looking in her eyes. "You know that, right?"

"Well, let me break it down for you, okay, so you have all the right information. I did try out for the Thug Heaven video. I did not screw anybody in Thug Heaven or on the set. I do not know why my sister is telling the whole school I'm a ho, or what made her tell my folks that Donald is gay. Well, Donald *is* gay, but still . . ."

"Who's Donald?"

Lauren's shoulders slumped; she pulled back from Jermaine's embrace. "Donald is my friend, is all."

"A friend, huh?"

"It's complicated," Lauren said, twirling onto his bed.

"Complicated, huh?"

"For the record, Jermaine, Donald *is* gay. And up until tonight, my parents thought he was my boyfriend."

"Now I'm really confused." Jermaine laughed as he sat down next to Lauren.

"I'm his beard, he's mine when I need him to be," Lauren said simply. "Or at least he was. His parents are shipping him off to boarding school on Monday."

This time, Jermaine contained his laughter. "Wow. Um, and you don't know why Sydney did all of this?"

"She's mad about something — probably her damn boyfriend. I just can't figure out why she can't take it out on him. It's not my fault he's a dog."

"But didn't you say he and Dara had something going on?"

"Yeah, but it wasn't a big deal, and I made sure that Dara ended it."

"So how you know your sister didn't know about it?"

Now as crazy as it sounds, this was the first time that Lauren had considered just how much intel her sister might have had on the Dara and Marcus situation. "Damn," she said.

"Look, Lauren, word is bond; your sister went out like a sucker if she sent that e-mail calling you a ho. But imagine if she really does know about the Dara situation? I mean, at the end of the day you can't care so much about what the people at your school think about you. You know what you are, and your sister does, too. And I'm guessing it's the same for any-body else who truly cares about you."

She didn't know what came over her when she did it, but just at that moment, Lauren leaned over and kissed Jermaine full on the lips — a soft, passionate one that said all the "thanks" she needed to convey. Jermaine returned it with a hearty "you're welcome," as the two of them fell back onto his bed, kissing and touching and kissing some more. Jermaine touched her face softly, then let his hands linger from her neck, down to her shoulder, and along the side of her body. She returned his passion with an embrace, inviting him into her mouth and wrapping her arms around his neck. Lauren hadn't had any intention of doing this; she truly went to Jermaine's house to talk — just talk. Not do this. But she couldn't help herself.

Still, when he climbed on top of her and she felt his fingers on her breasts, she got nervous. And when she heard shuffling in the living room just beyond Jermaine's bedroom door, she jumped up.

"I gotta get out of here," she said in a loud whisper.

Jermaine looked over at his digital alarm clock; it read 12:52 A.M. "Yeah, it's late, huh?"

"I need to get home," Lauren said, adjusting her shirt and tugging at her jeans. "Is that your brother out there?"

"Yeah," Jermaine said quietly. "Don't worry about him. Let's get your coat — I'm going to take you home."

155

"If you could just drop me off at the train station, I can get home from there. There's no way you'll be able to pull up into the driveway anyway," Lauren said. "The car will set off the sensors and Keisha will be all up in the monitors and dialing the police all in the same motion."

"Come on, now — this ain't the time or the neighborhood to be outside at this time of night. I'm going to drive you and drop you off at the end of your block and you can call my cell when you get inside. And don't bother saying no — I'm not having it any other way."

Lauren laughed. "Fine," she said. "But how are we going to get out of your house with your brother in the next room?"

"Who, Rodney? Please, that ain't nothing. He don't have nothing to do with me and how I handle mine," Jermaine said, sounding agitated.

"Okay," Lauren hesitated, clearly taken aback by Jermaine's sudden change in tone. "Well, um, let's get going," she said, looking at her watch nervously.

"Yeah, let's bounce."

Jermaine flung the door open, gave his brother a stare-down worthy of a scene in *The Wire*, and brushed past the chair he was sitting in. Lauren followed close behind, trying not to look too hard at Rodney.

"Well, well, baby brother, nice midnight snack," he said. "You sharing?"

Jermaine laughed, but clearly, his chuckle was not one meant to show he was humored. He started grinding his teeth; his temples bounced in circles. "Rodney, Lauren. Lauren, Rodney. She was just leaving," Jermaine said as he practically pushed Lauren toward the front door.

"What's the rush, baby brother?" Rodney asked, turning in his chair to face the couple. "Why don't you both stay and chat?"

Jermaine rolled his eyes and took Lauren's hand into his. He didn't say another word, just walked out into the autumn chill, Lauren in tow.

"Y'all come back now, ya hear?" Rodney called out as Lauren and Jermaine pushed through the door. "Maybe we can talk about getting me one of them Duke rides."

The door slammed.

Lauren wasn't sure if she heard it right, but it sounded like Rodney said her last name. *How does he know me*, she asked herself. She looked at Jermaine, but he didn't say anything. She wasn't even sure if he heard it.

But Lauren wasn't about to push the issue. Something about Rodney didn't set right with her. She wasn't about to start asking Jermaine questions about his brother, though; she didn't know him like that and was almost afraid of what he might say. Besides, Lauren just wanted to get back to Buckhead and pretend like this day never happened.

15
SYDNEY

"Actually, Caesar, you can just drop me off right here," Sydney requested in her sweetest voice as the car service pulled up at the bottom of her driveway.

"I would love to, miss, but my company has strict orders from your father to drop you off directly at the front door. No exceptions," Caesar explained apologetically as the black Cadillac Escalade continued up the long stretch to the main entrance of the Duke estate.

"Fine," Sydney huffed as she flopped back into her seat feeling more like a prisoner headed to the guillotine than the princess headed to her storybook castle.

In the seventy-two hours since Lauren dropped the bomb about Sydney's secret relationship with Dice, Altimus had literally snatched Sydney's life away. Her driving privileges, iPod, flat screen, and all phones were immediately confiscated. Weekly appointments at the spa, with the trainer, and her hairdresser were canceled indefinitely. The only thing Sydney was still allowed to do was eat, sleep, go to school, participate in after-school activities, and come straight home.

When Carmen and Rhea noticed Sydney getting dropped off by a car service on Monday morning, they were dying to know what was up. But honesty required spilling the beans about Dice. What would Rhea and Carmen, the daughters of two prominent lawyers, a psychologist, and a housewife, respectively, know about having a parent on lockdown? Instead, Sydney created a story about car issues and played it off as if she had requested the driver to avoid dealing with the responsibility of a loaner from her dad's dealership on the days that Marcus couldn't drive her. Luckily, the girls were too busy buzzing about Dara's "crazy" Boobgate rumors to bother prying any further.

"All right, miss, I'll see you tomorrow morning at seven-thirty sharp," Caesar announced as the SUV came to a stop.

"Mmm-hmm," Sydney replied as she hopped out and slammed the door shut. Even though she understood it wasn't Caesar's fault, his refusal to let her out before the Dukes' state-of-the-art surveillance camera caught her arrival still annoyed the hell out of her. Caesar waited patiently until

Sydney pulled out her keys and opened the front door before he drove off slowly.

Sydney stepped inside the foyer and closed the front door. "Hey, I'm home," she said to no one in particular as she dropped her bag and started taking off her gray Miu Miu ankle boots.

"Welcome home, Ms. Sydney," Edwina answered as she came around the corner.

"Hey, Edwina," Sydney replied halfheartedly as she noticed her car keys sitting in the bowl of keys on the foyer table. "Why's it so quiet around here?" At 4:45 P.M. on a Tuesday, the sound of her mom blasting *Access Hollywood* from the den was noticeably absent.

"Oh, Dr. Chin was a guest on the *Oprah* show this morning and his flight back from Chicago was delayed, so your mom's acupuncture appointment got pushed back," Edwina explained. "She probably won't be home for another two hours."

Sydney immediately straightened up. "Two hours?" she asked as if she didn't quite hear the elderly woman correctly the first time.

"Yes, miss, at least two hours."

Sydney started putting her boots back on as fast as she could. With her mom at the acupuncturist, Altimus working, and Lauren probably at practice, Edwina had just waved the green flag in Sydney's face. "Edwina, do me a favor? Can you please go upstairs and close my bedroom door?"

"Sure, no problem, miss . . ."

"Thanks. I'll be right back, I'm just gonna step out for a second, okay?" Sydney continued as she turned to grab the keys to her car. "But if anyone asks, the last thing you saw was me go up to my room. Okay?"

Edwina didn't even blink. "Of course, miss." She hadn't managed to keep her job at the Duke family estate for the past twelve years by not knowing when to mind her business.

"You're the best," Sydney thanked her as she hurried out the door. She had two unsupervised hours and she wasn't about to waste a minute. The front door barely closed before the sound of Sydney's car engine roared to life.

After forty minutes of aimless driving, Sydney pulled up to the back parking lot of Brookhaven. Ironically, of all the places she could be, this was the only one where she still felt like she still had some semblance of control over her life. She turned off the car, rested her head back against the headrest, and closed her eyes. She considered swinging by her Aunt Lorraine's or even the Boys Club, where Marcus was supposed to be volunteering until at least nine o'clock, but she quickly decided against it. A surprise visit was how she had gotten into this mess to begin with.

As the sound of Gwen Stefani's yodeling filled the car, Sydney felt the overwhelming sensation of despair pressing against her chest. She had nowhere to go and no one to turn to. Once again, Lauren had sold her down the river. Sydney thought about how angry Altimus and her mom were with her. She could still see the rage as it filled Altimus's face. In that moment, he had looked like a complete stranger to Sydney. She just couldn't understand why her parents were so hell-bent on keeping her from her father. She inhaled deeply to relieve the increasing pressure.

Just then a crowd of varsity football players spilled out of the gymnasium doors. Play fighting and yelling back and forth among themselves like a pack of frisky puppies, they headed toward the group of cars parked a few rows in front of Sydney.

"Aye, dog, I'm telling you. That little redbone from the skating rink is on it," asserted loudmouth Terrance.

"Yeah, yeah, yeah," Blue answered sarcastically. "Ain't that the same thing you said 'bout Trina before she played you short at the Fall Festival?"

"Yes, indeed, yes, indeed," laughed the group. As the boys drew closer, Sydney recognized Jason bringing up the rear of the crew. Unconsciously, she started tugging the gold hoop in her right earlobe.

"Say what you want, when I walk into the Homecoming dance with li'l mama on my arm, don't say shiiiiit!" Terrance countered with confidence as he clicked the car remote to his white BMW with ridiculous-looking rims. Three fellow players quickly pulled open the passenger doors and crowded in.

"We shall see, my man," laughed Shaun as he gave Jason a farewell handshake, opened the door to his Dodge Charger with the purple bowling ball paint, and motioned for Big Mo and Blue to join him.

"All right y'all, get home safe. Don't forget, extended practice tomorrow night. We got to get right for Homecoming," Jason reminded the remainder of the group as they all hopped in their respective vehicles. As team co-captain, he always chose to wait until everyone was situated with a ride before he headed out.

Sydney watched as Jason turned back and headed toward his truck. She hesitated as she weighed the pros and cons of getting his attention. It's not like she had anything important or specific to say. Truth be told, Sydney simply didn't feel like being alone. She took a quick peek in the vanity mirror. Once she verified that her makeup still looked fresh and her hair wasn't a complete wreck, Sydney made the sign of the cross and jumped out of her car. "Hey, Jason!" she called out brightly as he was getting into his truck. Jason stopped and turned at the sound of his name.

"What up, Syd?" he asked as a huge grin spread across his face.

"Nothing much," she replied as she headed over toward him. "Seems like I can't stop running into you these days, huh?"

"Yeah, you're right," he agreed as he closed his door and

leaned his back against the truck. He looked over at her Saab. "Funny, I don't remember seeing your car earlier today. I normally look for it when I get here in the morning."

"And why in the world would you be looking for my car? Jason Danden, you're not stalking me, are you?" Sydney teased as she finally reached his truck. She put her hand on her hip and tilted her head mischievously.

"Not at all. It's just that, normally, you and I are the first people to arrive . So I'm accustomed to seeing your Saab when I pull in," he replied easily and then paused to look Sydney in the eyes. "But if I was, would you be mad at me?"

Sydney hesitated at the loaded question. "Whatever, silly. So where are you headed in such a rush?"

"No rush, I'm just headed home. What about you? I didn't think there were any committee meetings this afternoon."

"Oh, no, I was out driving to kinda clear my head and ended up here. Weird right? You'd think I'd want to get as far away from this place as possible and instead . . ."

"Naw, I get it. It's like second nature," he said patting one of Sydney's flyaway curls back into place. The sensation from his touch made Sydney shiver. "You cold?"

"The temperature feels like it might be dropping," she said, trying to play off the goose bumps.

"You might be right," Jason said, although he looked like

he didn't believe her for one second. "Well, you want to sit in my truck? It's def warmer inside there."

"Um." Sydney looked around. At almost six o'clock, the place was pretty deserted. "Yeah, sure, why not."

Jason simply smiled and walked around to the passenger side to open the door for her to get inside. As he was closing her door, Sydney leaned over and returned the favor by opening the driver side door for him.

"I knew you were one of the great ones," he quipped as he got into the truck.

"Ah, *A Bronx Tale*," Sydney said softly, suddenly very aware that once again she was sitting in the star of the football team's truck.

"Don't laugh, but I love that movie," Jason admitted bashfully.

"No, I totally get you. I like the old movies, too. *Love Jones*, *The Best Man*, *Pretty Woman*, *Poetic Justice* . . ."

". . . *Set It Off*, *The Godfather*, *Boyz n the Hood*, *Dead Presidents*," he continued with a smile.

"I don't know about no *Boyz n the Hood*," Sydney said with a laugh. Once again, she was surprised at how easily they were able to talk and find things in common.

"Gotta say, I'm glad to see you laugh," Jason admitted. "You weren't really looking like yourself when I asked you what you were still doing here."

"Let's just say," Sydney said as she fidgeted with her Gucci horsebit ring, "it's been a long week."

"Dang, it's only Tuesday, Syd."

"Yeah, well, sometimes it's like that," she said softly as she thought about all the chaos swirling around her.

"Wanna talk about it? I mean you don't have to, but sometimes it helps," he offered sweetly as he gently placed a hand on top of Sydney's.

For the third time that day, Jason made Sydney hesitate. There was something about the gentleness of his voice, the warm pressure of his hand, and what felt like an honest interest in what was happening in her life that made her warm to him. She couldn't remember the last time Marcus had taken a genuine interest in what was happening to her if it didn't directly involve him or improve the status of their public profile as a couple. Not that Sydney wasn't guilty of her share of shadiness when it came to maintaining the perfect image. She just wished that sometimes he'd remember that there was an actual relationship that needed to be attended to beneath the facade. Sighing, Sydney slowly pulled her hand away. "It's okay. I think I'll figure it out."

Sensing the awkwardness of the moment, Jason straightened up. "Okay, well, my friends tell me I'm a good listener. If you ever need an ear, I'm here." He turned away and started up the truck. "Besides, the last time I checked, you still owed me a call," he joked as he put the truck in reverse and brought it up alongside Sydney's car with ease.

"Very nice." Sydney opted to compliment his driving skills instead of answering his question. "The last time Lauren threw her car into reverse, she almost backed into a tree."

"Yeah, no offense, but I heard your sister goes through cars like underwear," he replied good-naturedly.

Sydney snorted. "Please, no offense taken. If you knew what I've been through with my sister, you'd know that calling her a bad driver is the least."

Jason chuckled. "Yeah, seems like siblings can be a trip. All my boys who have brothers and sisters stay bellyaching about them."

"Is that so?" Sydney asked sarcastically. She couldn't imagine anyone dealing with as much grief as Lauren constantly caused.

"Yep, yep. But take it from an only child, when push comes to shove, no one gets down for the get-down like family."

Sydney briefly considered his words. "I guess," she said quietly.

Jason reached out and softly touched Sydney's face. "Don't guess, know."

16
LAUREN

"You're not scared, are you?" Jermaine asked Lauren as he filled a glass with ice and stuck it under the rush of water coming out of the kitchen-sink tap.

"Uh, first of all, don't insult the kid like that — ain't nobody skerd of your friends," Lauren giggled as she reached around Jermaine's waist for the water glass.

Of course, she was lying; the evil looks she got from that girl the time she met Jermaine's friends at the mall were not lost on her, and it was crystal he was afraid to bring her around them, too, because over the past few weeks during their clandestine love affair, he avoided meeting her in his neighborhood at all costs. They'd always show up somewhere neutral, where people were too preoccupied with their own doings to pay too much attention to theirs — Piedmont Park in the middle of Atlanta, where they strolled hand-in-hand and rolled down the expansive hills set against the silvery Atlanta skyline; the Georgia Aquarium, where mothers pushed their strollers past the smooching couple as they shared a kiss in front of the dancing beluga whales; Fat Matt's, where they licked the barbeque sauce off their fingers with abandon — without a care in the world who was looking, because there was no reason for anyone either of them knew to be in any of those places. They liked it that way; that anonymity gave them the opportunity to show each other who they really were, without being forced to color in the lines that their friends, their families, and even they had created for themselves. But this playing with his friends plan? Extra.

"I'm just saying, why we gotta go to a pool hall and hang out with your friends when we can stay here and enjoy some quality alone-time?"

Jermaine turned around slowly so that the front of his body was pressed directly against hers. Lauren could feel his breath on her cheek. "Because when my moms gets home in a half hour, we won't be alone and it certainly won't be enjoyable," Jermaine said, leaning down to kiss her lips.

"Well, if I had the choice between meeting your mother or your friends, I'd go with your mom. I mean, I don't exactly have on the proper gaming attire," Lauren said, looking down at her tight metallic V-neck BCBG sweater, Earl Jean pencil skirt, and black patent-leather Bottega Veneta peep-toe pumps. Clearly, she was reaching. "And why you hiding me from your mother, anyway? What? — I'm not good enough to meet her?"

Jermaine kicked his game into high gear; he knew that the next few words out of his mouth had to be convincing enough to get Lauren out of the house *now*, because it was only a matter of time before his mother came back from the parole office with Rodney, and there was no way he could have the daughter of Altimus Duke standing in the middle of the living room when they arrived. After all, Rodney had made it clear that if Jermaine didn't tell her, he would.

And that Jermaine wasn't about to have.

"Look," he said, kissing Lauren's lips between every few words. "I want you to meet my moms, for real. But she ain't really going to appreciate walking into her house and seeing you sitting in her kitchen, spending what she might misinterpret as quality alone-time with her son while she's not in the house. That would not be a pretty scene, trust."

Lauren looked into his eyes and smiled. She, of course, could understand the dilemma. It wasn't like she could invite Jermaine over to her house for tea and crumpets, either, not with Altimus and Keisha standing in the foyer. She conjured up an image of her parents opening the double wrought-iron doors, Altimus with his arms folded, Keisha with her lips pursed, zoning in on his sagging pants and white T, ready to frisk him for weapons and send him packing once they decided he didn't have the right addy and daddy. Especially since the whole Donald-is-gay-thing, which, at first, her parents didn't want to believe — until, that is, Keisha happened upon a letter Donald sent from his new boarding school. It started: "Dear L, My God, I thought I would hate your sister forever for pulling me out the closet, but my 'punishment' at this all-boys' school has turned into quite the tasty treat. Tell Syd I said thanks!"

Yeah, Keisha wasn't exactly trusting of Lauren's judgment or taste in men these days (though Lauren had done enough fast-talking to make her parents believe she was just as clueless about Donald's sexual status as they were). Anyway, Lauren quickly decided that she should probably stop pushing the "I wanna meet your mom" issue with Jermaine, seeing as there was no way in hell she was going to be hosting her own "meet the parents" soiree anytime soon. He had to remain her secret, for now. And this she wasn't ready to explain to Jermaine. Better to go and be uncomfortable standing around a bunch of thug Negroes for an hour or so than have that conversation. "Fine. Let's go meet your little friends. But don't get there and forget who you came with," she warned. "You should know that I don't like sharing."

"Is that right?" Jermaine said, planting another gentle kiss on her lips. "Well, I have no intentions of sharing this right here." He squeezed Lauren's butt and kissed her again. "That's all me."

The word "uncomfortable" was a gross understatement of how Lauren felt walking hand-in-hand with Jermaine into The Playground, a small hole-in-the-wall neighborhood haunt nestled between a small independent music store (where in addition to mix tapes and bootleg rap CDs, they sold everything a modern Negro could want: white Ts, sports jerseys, caps, sneakers, and a wide assortment of gold fronts) and a fried-fish joint called Pride, where she and Jermaine waited behind no less than a dozen people to buy a four-dollar basket of crispy fried tilapia piled high on top of three pieces of white bread (the fish made Lauren's mouth water, but she was ticked that she'd have to find a way to get that smell out of her top). Suffice to say that her man's friends didn't exactly roll out the Welcome Wagon when Lauren, freshly introduced by Jermaine as "my girl," shined her high-wattage grin in their direction, hoping her big butt and friendly smile would be disarming enough for them to treat her like she belonged.

Not so much.

"What up, Pimpin'?" Jermaine said, slapping hands and snapping fingers with a guy he introduced as Don.

"Yeah, man, what's really hood?" Don said, half smiling as he stared Lauren up and down. He looked back at the crowd of his boys and their various ill-dressed chicks who seemingly adored them; they were assembled around the pool table, pretending to be waiting for or watching the game action, but really what they were doing was peeping Lauren.

The pressure made her ears hot; the smell of the fish grease on her hands made her nauseous. She wanted — needed — to make a speedy exit, but then how would she look running through the hood in four-inch heels and a $200 glitter sweater? Her guess was it wouldn't end well.

So she chilled. Or at least tried to.

"Where you been, man? We ain't seen you round in a while," Don said, his eyes shifting back and forth between Jermaine and Lauren.

"Aw, man, you know — just maintaining, doing my thing," Jermaine said.

"I can see that, blood. Can definitely see that," Don said, his eyes strolling slowly up from Lauren's shoes to her eyes.

Lauren tried not to shiver. She nearly jumped out of her skin when a group of boys shooting dice in the far right corner, near the video machines, started hollering, laughing, and slap-snapping each other's hands, presumably over one player's lucky roll. "Um, Jermaine, I'm going to go over to the bar area over there and get some water — you want anything?" she asked quickly.

She heard the girls sucking their teeth and got a mental image of them rolling their eyes behind her back.

"I'll get it for you — you want bottled or tap?" Jermaine asked as she started walking to the bar.

"No, no — it's cool, I'll go get it," Lauren practically snapped.

"I'll go with her," one of the girls chimed in, stepping forward. "I'm Brandi." She said her name sweetly, but the look on her face read something else altogether: bitch. "Come on, leave the boys to their game."

Lauren tossed a look at Jermaine, who just shrugged. "Take care of my girl," Jermaine said half-jokingly, his eyes showing his worry. Brandi didn't bother answering him back. Don shoved a pool stick in his hand and motioned Jermaine over to the pool table.

"So," Brandi said without looking at Lauren. "What's your name again?"

"Uh, Lauren."

"You have a last name, Lauren?"

"It's um, Duke," Lauren said, clearing her throat, making it sound like she wasn't really sure if her answer was correct. "Duke," she said more confidently.

"Stone!" Brandi yelled at a guy standing in the storeroom behind the register. The bass in her voice startled Lauren, who instantly turned her head and looked back for Jermaine. He paid her no nevermind; Jermaine was already knee-deep into his pool game. "Hey, Stone! Let me get a Coke and a bottled water!" She turned to Lauren: "Let's sit here by the door; the vent is over here — it's warmer."

Lauren looked back at Jermaine again; he waved and went back to his stance over the pool table, taking aim at the yellow-striped ball. Brandi sat on a rickety stool at the bar and motioned for Lauren to take the stool next to her. Lauren obliged.

Brandi didn't waste any time getting to the matter at hand. "So, you and Jermaine, how'd y'all meet?"

Lauren cleared her throat. "We, um, we met while I was visiting some relatives over here in the West End."

"You got people livin' around here?" Brandi asked, wrinkling her eyebrows. Stone dropped the Coke and water on the counter and swiped up the three dollars Brandi had left for him.

"Yeah, um, I have an aunt who lives here."

"I see."

"He's a really nice guy — how do you know him?"

"Who, Jermaine?" Brandi asked, chuckling. "Oh, we go way back. We grew up here together, even dated for a minute or two."

Lauren nearly choked on her Crystal Springs.

"What? — you didn't think he had females before you?" Brandi asked coolly as she sipped her soda. "Oh, there've been plenty others. Let's just say that Jermaine is one of the hot boys around here. But it ain't just because of his looks, you know."

Now just what in the hell was that supposed to mean? Lauren asked herself (she knew better than to say that out loud). She took another sip of water and kept quiet. Under normal circumstances, on her own turf, she might have had a few choice words to say, but, most def, she needed to feel this chick out. *Oh, who am I fooling?* Lauren asked herself. *This broad would beat my ass. Let me shut up.*

"He used to always go around talking about how he was going to get up out the hood and do some things didn't nobody expect from him," Brandi continued. "From the looks of things, he sho wasn't lying," she said, rolling her eyes at Lauren and turning back to her Coke.

"I'm sorry?" Lauren said, swizzing her neck.

"Don't be sorry, honey, Jermaine is a catch," Brandi snapped. "But I'm just letting you know that there were a lot of girls before you and there will be a lot more after you so don't think you're going to get comfortable on the West End because bitches like you come a dime a —"

Lauren's eyes grew wider with every word that tumbled from Brandi's lips, but when she called her a bitch, it was on.

"Look here, I don't know who you callin' bitch, but I do know you need to watch how you speak to *this* bitch," Lauren practically growled, getting up from her stool. "I'm not from around here, but you not gonna sit up here and talk to me any ol' kinda way, I know that much . . ."

Lauren kept going, curses flying every which way from her mouth — words that she wasn't quite sure she could back up but sounded good anyway. Must have, because with every tidbit that tumbled from her lips, Brandi's eyes grew wider and wider. Lauren wasn't sure if she was reading her nemesis's face right, but she could have sworn on her grandmother's grave that Brandi looked, well, scared. Lauren, all at once surprised and pleased by Brandi's reaction, was ready to go in for the kill — to stand up and stick a finger or two in Brandi's face for emphasis. But just as she raised her hands, she realized that Brandi's fearful eyes weren't focused on her; Brandi was looking past Lauren — over her shoulder and toward the door.

It was exactly at that moment that Lauren felt the chill through her sweater. She turned around to see who was walking in the door, sure that she was about to be hurt by someone presenting himself to rob the club and everyone in it. But what she saw was worse. Much worse. Her eyes settled on Altimus, who was right in the middle of telling somebody off. She considered rubbing her eyes to make sure they weren't playing tricks on her, but she didn't need to: Her stepdad, the epitome of grace, elegance, and composure, was in the hood straight looking like a gangsta all up in some old man's face.

"Look here, mufucka, I ain't gonna say this but one time, so listen good . . ." Altimus said through his teeth, pushing his fingers into the face of a man who was sitting a few stools away from Lauren. Just as he was about to really lay into the guy, he caught a glimpse of Lauren out of the corner of his eye. He straightened his shoulders; his eyes, narrowed like slits, locked with his daughter's.

"What the hell are you doing here?" he asked her through clenched teeth.

Busted. Unsure whether to answer Altimus's question, or ask him one, Lauren settled on stammering. "I-I-," she started.

"I — I hell. I asked you a question, Lauren. Who you with up in here?" he demanded, looking at Brandi and then the crowd of teenagers gathered in the area around the pool table. A hush fell over the club; not one person in the place so much as blinked. Lauren could hear two things: Altimus's breathing, heavy with anger, and her own heartbeat. Jermaine took a small step forward, but Don put a firm hand on his shoulder, a silent warning not to get in the middle of this mess.

"You know what? I don't even want to hear that shit right now. Get your ass up and go get in the car."

"But — " Lauren started.

"I. Said. Get. Your. Ass. In. The. Car. Lauren," Altimus said through his teeth, grabbing Lauren by the arm and practically pulling her off the stool. Lauren lost her footing as she stepped down, making her left heel topple over. It hurt like hell, but she resisted yelping — just limped through the door. Altimus's fingers gripped her arm so tightly, she thought for sure he'd stopped its blood flow.

The door slammed behind the two, the rattling of the glass and the chimes on top of it making everyone in the place jump.

After a few seconds, Brandi got up and peeped out the window, watching as Altimus practically threw Lauren into the front seat of his gunmetal-gray 7 Series. She didn't take her eyes off the scene until Altimus screeched away.

"Oh, shit — Jermaine? What you done did?" Brandi yelled, turning on her heels to face the sea of white T's that had gathered just beyond her. "What the hell were you thinking?"

"For real, dude, you know who you messin' wit?" Don asked, shaking his head, murmurs of "yo," and "oh, shit" filling the air.

"Come on, man, I know who she is," Jermaine shrugged. "It ain't no thang."

"I know you know who she is, son. Do you know who her daddy is, that's the question," Don said.

"I know who he is, too, you ain't sayin' nothin' right now," Jermaine said confidently.

"Oh, I ain't sayin' shit, huh? You know who he is, huh? You know that he is the biggest gangsta in the West End? And you messin' with his fam — his baby girl? Yo, I gotta give it to you nephew, that's gangsta. But *you* ain't no gangsta. Best leave that up to your big brother, baby boy. Unless you ready to deal with that gangsta shit, fo real," Don said, raising his hands in surrender.

"I keep tellin' you, ain't no thang," Jermaine said, almost as if he were trying to reassure himself, as much as his friends. "Me and Lauren cool. I ain't worried about Altimus Duke."

Don just looked at Jermaine and then his boys and shook his head. He stared at Jermaine some more. "I tell you what, nephew — you best to worry. For real. That man right there? You ain't ready for him."

17
SYDNEY

"So, any idea when your dad is going to give back your driving privileges?" Marcus asked hesitantly as he turned off the ignition. With only a few minutes until first bell, the parking lot was crowded with cars and students.

"He's my *step*father," Sydney countered as she pulled the collar on her heavyweight Catherine Malandrino cardigan tighter around her neck. At 7:45 in the morning, the sun hadn't been up long enough to burn off the fall chill in the morning air. The last thing Sydney wanted to do was fool around and get a sore throat right before Homecoming week. "And no, I don't. Why? What's the problem, you already tired of driving me? 'Cause if there's someone else that you need to be picking up . . ."

"I'm just asking a question, Sydney. You don't have to

be so defensive," Marcus replied as he grabbed his black suede jacket from the backseat. "I know you're upset because of what happened at dinner, but I told you that I don't want to fight with you. I'm on your side, remember?"

"I guess," Sydney mumbled miserably as she looked out the window. Karina and Karma Bedders, one of Brookhaven's three sets of identical twins, waved in greeting as they passed Marcus's car on their way into the building. Sydney smiled weakly in return.

"So what do you think your mom is going to do, now that she knows?" Marcus questioned. "I don't think I've ever seen her that angry. And not to be judgmental, but do you really think it's a good idea for you to be hanging out with a — "

"With a what, Marcus? An ex-con? A gun smuggler? My biological father?"

"That's not what I meant and you know it. I'm just playing devil's advocate. I want you to get to know your dad, but I don't want you to get hurt in the process."

"I can't even believe you right now, Marcus. You of all people know how long I've wanted my father to be in my life and now you say all of this?"

Marcus rubbed his chin as he contemplated his next words. "All I'm saying, Syd, is that it's one thing to send the man letters. It's a whole other thing to be hanging out in the hood. Is it really worth it?"

As Sydney watched Marcus rifle through his book bag, she felt like she was looking at a complete stranger. Marcus was the only person whom Sydney had ever trusted enough to tell her complete family history. How could he even question whether it was worth it?

"Hey, like I said, I'm on your side," he insisted, cutting off her thoughts with a quick peck on the lips. "Anyway, before I forget, my mom is being honored by the Association of Nuevo Black Socialites the fifteenth of next month."

"Well, isn't that just special," Sydney deadpanned as she thought about how much her own mother aspired to belong to the exclusive group of affluent, well-connected, and extremely powerful Atlanta housewives. Unfortunately, all the money in the world couldn't hide the hood in Keisha, and the Nuevo Black Socialites weren't having it.

"I guess. She expects us to be there so mark your calendar. Oh, and why don't you wear your hair up in twists? I like it so much better that way," he stated as he turned to open the driver side door.

"Yes'm, boss," Sydney muttered under her breath.

"What'd you say?" Marcus questioned as he turned around.

"Nothing, nothing. I said fine," Sydney offered as she started to open her own door and suddenly sat back in her seat.

"You coming, Syd? We're going to be late and you know I have Dr. Daniels for first." Marcus impatiently beckoned.

"Actually," Sydney started slowly as she formed the story in her mind. "I really need to go get something that I forgot at home."

"Huh? You wanna go home? Sydney, what are you talking about?" Marcus asked with a facial expression caught somewhere between annoyance and confusion.

"I, um, I just remembered that I have a presentation this afternoon and I left my note cards at home. I really need to go get them. Can I please borrow your car?"

"What about your first period? Are you just going to cut class?" Marcus asked incredulously.

"Marcus, please. Re-lax, I'm coming right back. Besides, I've got independent study with Ms. Korkow for two periods this morning. You act like I've never driven your car before. It'll be fine," Sydney explained as her voice became more assertive. "I promise."

Marcus paused and looked across the parking lot as the number of remaining students steadily decreased. The first bell sounded. "Fine," he sighed, holding out the keys. "Just hold on to the keys until I see you at lunch."

As she leaned across the driver seat to grab the keys, Sydney pulled Marcus back into the BMW. "Love you," she whispered as she gave him a quick kiss.

"Uh-huh, just be careful with my car. I don't need both of us to be without wheels," he replied as he pulled away and started jogging toward the school's entrance without a backward glance.

"Blah, blah, blah," Sydney muttered as she hopped over to the driver's side and closed the door. At the moment, Sydney didn't have the time or energy to pay Marcus's comment any attention. She had exactly an hour and a half to get across town to her Aunt Lorraine's house and back before third period began. She couldn't afford to skip a single AP Geometry class if she wanted to keep her GPA above a 3.8 this semester.

Thirty minutes later, Sydney pulled into her Aunt Lorraine's driveway. Although it was almost eight-thirty in the morning, all the shades were tightly drawn. Clearly no one in this house started his or her day before noon.

As she hurried up the walkway, Sydney stepped lightly over the uneven and crumbling pavement. The sound of Jerry Springer blasted out of the neighbor's bedroom window. Sydney crinkled her nose in disgust as she passed a fresh pile of steaming dog crap.

"Who dat?" her Aunt Lorraine called out as Sydney rang the doorbell for the third time.

"It's me, Aunt Lorraine. It's Sydney," she replied in relief. For a second, Sydney worried that she'd come all the way across town for nothing.

"Chile, where you been? You know your poor daddy was worried sick when he hadn't heard from you all these days. You ain't in no trouble is you?" Aunt Lorraine scolded as she opened the door. "No matter, just come on in and have a seat. I'll go fetch him from the back bedroom right quick."

"Thanks, Aunt Lorraine," Sydney answered as she headed into the living room. She could hear her aunt banging on the bedroom door and telling her father to get up because his daughter was waiting to see him.

Moments later, Dice walked into the living room wearing a pair of red-and-green-plaid pajama bottoms, a white Sean John logo T-shirt, and the pair of leather slippers Sydney had sent him a couple of years ago for Christmas. He immediately headed over to Sydney and scooped her up in a tight hug. "Where ya been, Ladybug? I was starting to get worried about you. I sent you a bunch of text messages but none of them were returned. So then I called your cell, but it said that the number was temporarily out of service. Everything straight?"

"Oh, Dad, everything is all messed up. Dara slept with Marcus and Lauren knew about it, so I told everyone about Lauren's video ho tryout and Dara's boobs, then that backstabber told Mom that I'd been coming here to see you, so Altimus put me on punishment after I outted gay-ass Donald at dinner," Sydney exclaimed breathlessly before she burst into tears.

"Whoa, whoa, Ladybug, slow down. Now, who slept with Marcus? And Lauren's a video what? When did Keisha get fake boobs? And why is Altimus putting his hands on my child?" Dice asked, clearly confused. He rubbed Sydney on the back to try and soothe her sobs.

"No, Dad, Mom didn't get fake boobs," she said in between sniffles. "Lauren's slutty best friend slept with Marcus. I think. I mean, obviously he's denying it. Shoot, he even denied that they were hanging out together and I found proof of that. Anyway, I'd never give her the satisfaction of admitting that I think my man would ever stoop to her level, but something just ain't right between the two of them. And I'm pissed."

"Seems like you have every right to be mad, Syd," Dice answered knowingly as he steered her toward the couch. He stopped on the way to grab a handful of Kleenex from a box by Aunt Lorraine's easy chair and handed them to Sydney.

"Well, what made me really, really, pissed is that if Dara did get with Marcus, Lauren totally knew about the whole thing," Sydney said as she loudly blew her nose into the tissue.

"Whoa. You sure about that?"

"Positive," she asserted. "So since they both stabbed me in the back, I figured I'd get them back where it hurts. I sent an e-mail to this blog that like everyone in the whole world reads, about the fact that Lauren didn't make the cut at a video tryout and that Dara's mom used child-support money to get Dara a boob job."

"Hold up now — what exactly is your sister trying to do in videos? And what in the world is a blog? You lost me, babe . . ."

"Oh, please, Lauren is such a wannabe tramp," Sydney blurted out. "She's been hanging out with Dara, sneaking around doing crazy things like, forever. I don't understand how our parents — I mean Mom and Altimus — haven't figured out her Little Miss Cheerleader act yet, but whatever. Don't even worry about the blog. Let's just say I put Lauren and Dara on major blast. So to get back at me, Lauren told Mom that I've been coming over here to see you."

"Damn," Dice muttered. He may not have understood much of anything else, but he damn sure knew what that last statement meant.

"Exactly," Sydney said with a frustrated frown as the tears started to well up once again. "She put me on blast in the middle of dinner right in front of her stupid boyfriend, Donald."

"Who's gay?" Dice questioned, shaking his head in disbelief.

"Yep, pretty much. But that's nothing compared to how Mom and Altimus lost it when they heard about you and me. Mom was ranting and raving like a lunatic. I swear if looks could kill, I'd be dead right now."

"Yeah, I remember those cut eyes your mother used to give me."

"Which, to be honest, I totally don't understand the reason for. Why is Mom so hell-bent on keeping me away from you? And P.S., why does Altimus care so much all of a sudden? He went off and punished me like I'd crashed one of his vintage cars or something. Oh, wait, Lauren already did that last year." Sydney snickered evilly as she wiped her runny nose. "You know what? Even then, all he did was ground her for a week. I, on the other hand, am grounded indefinitely."

Dice took a deep breath as he reached out for Sydney's trembling hand. "The more I listen to you, the more convinced I am that this whole situation is rigged all the way around. There are a lot of things that you can't understand because you don't know your past," he said slowly.

"Huh? What are you talking about, Dad?"

"Listen, Syd," he said. "You know I've always said that I was innocent of the charges that I was convicted of, right? But I wasn't an innocent man. Back in the day, I was definitely in the streets . . . in a big way. I made a lot of enemies, apparently even among those people that were the closest to me."

"Okay . . ." Sydney encouraged him to continue.

"It's . . ." Dice paused. "You just have to believe me when I tell you that everything you've been told about me, my relationship with your mother and why things turned out the way they are — isn't necessarily true."

"Well, I knew that," Sydney started. "But that doesn't explain why Mom gets so crazy. What does she think is gonna happen if I spend time with you?"

"One thing you have to understand about your mother is that she's not the chick that's going to lose. If she feels threatened, she will lash out to maintain whatever she feels is her rightful position."

"So what, she thinks she's gonna lose me to you or something?" Sydney questioned, even more confused.

"Maybe," Dice continued bitterly. "I mean, think about it, Syd. If I was really such a horrible person, then she should have no problem bringing you girls around the way. 'Cause everyone would know how terrible I was and be on her side, wouldn't they? But instead, your mother keeps the two of you cut off from everyone who might know the real deal. Me, my family, shoot — she don't even bring you guys around her own family no more."

"I guess I never thought about that. Since Grammy and Grampy died when we were little . . ."

"But what about your Uncle Laurence? Your mother's own brother? Lauren is named after that man, and I'll bet you probably never heard his name before today."

Uncle Laurence? My mother has a brother? She felt like the wind had been knocked out of her.

Dice simply looked down at his hands in response. "I'm right aren't I?" he insisted.

"You have to tell me what is going on," Sydney urged her father.

"It's not for me to tell you bad things about your mother, Sydney. I've already said too much. You just need to be careful and pay attention. I don't want you to get hurt."

Hearing her father repeat the same exact words Marcus had said to her earlier rattled Sydney to the core. Her legs shook like leaves as she struggled to stand. "I-I-I have to go. I need to get back," she stuttered as she stumbled toward the front door.

"Sydney . . ."

"No, I can't," Sydney pushed past her dad and ran out the door. She jumped in the car and threw it in reverse so fast she almost hit the lopsided mailbox that leaned into the driveway. As she sped off down the road, Dice stood in the doorway, rubbing his head and hoping with all his heart that he'd done the right thing.

18
LAUREN

Dara pushed her way out of the locker room with a quick "see ya later," and not so much as a sideways glance at Lauren. Honestly, Lauren didn't know how much longer she was supposed to take her best friend's abuse; she'd apologized to her on several occasions, even though she didn't really have anything to do with the whole e-mail debacle, and even had gone on youngrichandtriflin.com to defend the two of them, clarifying the whole video tryout rumor — *My agent did suggest I try out for the Thug Heaven video, but when I arrived on the set, I quickly determined it just wasn't my scene and I left without auditioning*, she'd written, insisting that, *to the best of my knowledge, Dara's private parts are all her own and nobody's business but her own.* While it seemed like the rest of the school had lightened up and moved on, Dara was still hang-ing on to the mess like a two-year-old in a dirty diaper.

Lauren was over it.

Besides, she had much bigger concerns, namely the fall-out after Altimus caught her in the West End. It had not been pretty. From the moment he snatched her from the pool hall, Altimus had been laying into her with questions about why she was there, who she was seeing, what she knew about the neighborhood, if she was there trying to find her father's fam-ily, like her sister. "Come on now, Daddy, you know I don't want anything to do with that man or his relations," Lauren had insisted as she slumped down in the front seat of Altimus's ride, her shades hiding both her fear and embarrassment of having been snatched up.

"Then what were you doing here?"

"I told you, I have a few friends in that neighborhood and I just dropped by to hang out for a while," Lauren insisted.

"You just dropped by, huh?"

"Yes — just like you," Lauren snapped, gathering up a little courage to ask Altimus what he was doing there, cussing out folks and looking real regular. Altimus had already made a point of saying he was there for "business purposes," but what car dealership business would have him jabbing his fin-ger in somebody's face and cursing like he was? "Didn't look like a business call to me," Lauren huffed.

"I'm a grown-ass man with multiple businesses around Georgia, and if I need to be in the West End, I most certainly don't need to check in with you to do so," Altimus sneered.

"No disrespect, but that's how I feel about the company I keep," Lauren said, her heart racing. "I don't need to check in with you or my mother about my friends, and I most certainly am capable of making a few outside of the exclusive little group you and Keisha force on me."

"Force on you? Force on you? Little girl, let me tell you something," Altimus seethed, abruptly pulling the BMW to the side of the road, a screech of the brakes punctuating his anger. He slammed on the breaks so hard, Lauren's head jerked forward and then crashed back against the butter-soft black leather headrest. Altimus threw the car in park and then jerked his body around to face Lauren. He leaned into her face so close, she could feel his hot breath on her cheeks. "You don't know a damn thing about force," he practically whispered, his words giving way only to his heavy breathing. "But I sure can show it to you, little girl. You want to see some force in action?"

Lauren tried to back away, but there was nowhere for her to go — her head was already lying against the cold glass of the passenger window. The fire in Altimus's eyes made her fingers go icy. Her stepfather was scaring the crap out of her.

"What? — Can't speak now?" Altimus said, leaning in closer still. "See you real quick at the lip, but let me tell you something, you little smart-mouthed brat: You don't want no part of this. What I do in the West End is my business. Grown-folk business. Stay the hell out of it, got me?"

"Y-yes," Lauren stammered.

Altimus stared into Lauren's eyes a beat longer and then slowly leaned back into his own seat. He reached into his ashtray and grabbed an old cigar he'd stubbed out before he walked into the pool hall earlier. He lit it, then puffed a few times, all the while looking through the front windshield.

"Now," he said calmly. "Hand over your cell phone, don't even think about driving Sydney's car, and outside of school and after-school functions, don't even think about going anywhere other than home."

Under normal circumstances, Lauren would have protested the lockdown, but something told her to keep her mouth shut, lest Altimus pop her in it.

"And one more thing," he added, finally turning to look at her again. "Reach into the glove compartment, take out a pen and a piece of paper, and write down the names of everybody you know in the West End."

"But — " Lauren started.

"But, hell," Altimus yelled, slamming his hands down on the steering wheel. "Write them."

Lauren jumped at the sound of Altimus's hands against the wheel. "Okay," she said, "but I only know first names. I barely know them."

Altimus puffed on his cigar. "That's all I need."

And this is why the very next day, Lauren found herself rushing to the computer lab after school to IM Jermaine. Her phone confiscated and both her and Sydney's computers down in the kitchen where Keisha and Altimus could keep close tabs on their usage, she had no other choice but to fight off the geeks in the computer room to get the message to Jermaine that her father may be looking for him. More important, though, she wanted — needed — to see him. Lauren checked her watch; she had no more than five minutes to run up to her locker, switch out her books, check her lip gloss, and run back down to the computer room to send Jermaine a short IM. Lauren took the steps two by two, weaving between kids laughing and playing around in the hallway as they made their way to the buses and cars and extracurricular activities. She hardly heard Marcus calling her name, so consumed was she with getting to where she needed to be.

"Lauren!" Marcus shouted a little louder. He rushed up to her and put his hand on her shoulder. "Hold up a sec, I need to talk to you."

Ugh. The scent of his musty-ass hair filled her nose before she fully understood what he asked her. "What?" she said, annoyed.

"Listen, I need to talk to you," he said, looking around to see if anyone was watching.

"Marcus, I'm in a rush — I don't have time to chat," Lauren said as she began to walk away.

Marcus's grip got a little tighter; Lauren looked at her shoulder and then at Marcus, who, after seeing the look in her eyes, quickly moved his hand off Lauren's body. "I really need to talk to you," he pleaded. "It's important."

"Go," Lauren said, rolling her eyes and shifting from one foot to the other.

"I need to set things straight with Sydney and the only way I can do that is with your help."

"Oh, Negro, please . . ."

"Wait, hear me out," Marcus insisted. "She's been treating me like crap lately and I feel like we've built too much over these past four years for it all to go down the drain."

"And what, exactly, does all of this have to do with me, Marcus?" Lauren huffed, checking her watch. "I mean, you lie down with dogs, you come up with fleas. Sounds like Sydney's just itching. If you ask me, it's about time."

Marcus let out a sigh. "Look, Lauren, I know you think I'm about the bullshit. But I really love your sister and I don't want to lose her, especially over Dara."

Dara? Now Lauren's ears perked up. "Go on."

Marcus, oblivious, continued. "Look, I need you to give Dara a message. I'd tell her myself, but if Sydney catches me within a hundred-foot radius of the girl, she'll lose it, and frankly, she's already on the edge. I don't want to be the one to push her over it. Just tell Dara that I said Sydney knows all about our relationship and it has to come to an end — it's over."

"What's over?" Lauren said, confused.

"Me and Dara."

"You and Dara?" Lauren asked.

"Come on, Lauren — me and Dara. Don't make me have to spell it all out for you. I know Dara's told you all about us. She's your best friend, for Christ's sake. Just tell her for me that what we had between us is o-v-e-r. Tell her to stop calling me, stop trying to come over to the house, stop showing up at my volunteer functions, my classes, leaving notes in my locker. Just stop it all. I need to focus on Sydney now, and I can't have her shadowing me, screwing up things even more between me and my girlfriend — your sister. Enough. What we had together is over."

Lauren was flabbergasted — had no words. This was her sister's boyfriend standing here telling her that the girl she considered her best friend in the entire world was creeping with her twin's man? Right up under her nose? Seriously? For the first time since that night at the High, Lauren was learning of the true extent of Dara's deceit. It was one thing to kiss Marcus, but have an entire hot-and-heavy hookup relationship? And then practically stalk him like she was ready to take Sydney's place? What the hell?

What was so bad about it, Lauren thought, was that Dara was stomping around Brookhaven Prep like Lauren had done *her* wrong. And all this time, Lauren was trying to think up ways to get it back to the way it was before all the drama. Now she knew the answer: It wasn't going to happen. No way.

And God, what must Sydney be thinking?

"Marcus," Lauren said, "Sydney is your girlfriend, not mine. Anything you got going on in your little love triangle is your business, not mine. Now if you'll excuse me," she said, pushing past him.

Lauren ran over to the window to get a good look at the pick-up circle; the black Benz was there waiting, the driver leaning against the front bumper, alternately checking his watch and looking at the front door for his charge. He could wait, Lauren quickly decided as she pushed past Marcus and headed for the computer lab. She rushed in, only to find all the computers taken. She rolled her eyes and shook her head at all the geeks leaning into the screens, oblivious to the fact that, after school, the rest of the world actually lived their lives while they sat mesmerized by their stupid little computer games and homework and whatever else it was that they did on those machines. She quickly surveyed the room and scoped out the ugliest, corniest boy she could find and sauntered up to him. "Hey there, cutie, what you working on?" she asked sweetly. The boy practically fell out of his chair.

"Um, uh, I'm, uh, just doing a little homework," he gushed goofily.

"Well, I was hoping you could help me out. I need to send a quick IM to a friend of mine and all of the other computers are taken. Can I use yours? Just for a sec?" she asked, leaning into the boy so close he could smell what she had for lunch.

"Su-sure," the boy stuttered as he got up clumsily from his chair. "It's all yours."

Lauren's fingers flew across the keys as she logged into her Yahoo account and IM'd Jermaine.

"I really need to talk to you. I'm breathless — been waiting for you," she wrote.

Her computer rang out almost instantly.

"Breathe!" followed by a smiley face.

"It's about my dad," she wrote. "It's kinda hectic around here, but I need to be around someone sane. You won't believe what I just found out. I need to see you."

"You're on the lockdown — I'll send a picture."

Lauren laughed. "I'm on the lockdown between school hours and bedtime. Nobody said anything about midnight."

"Midnight? What U got in mind?"

"Just meet me at the spot. Midnight. Gotta run. Be careful."

By the time Lauren made it to the car — a good fifteen

minutes after she was supposed to be there — the driver had a serious attitude, but Lauren didn't really give a crap. As she approached, she put her sunglasses on and stood at the back passenger side of the vehicle, waiting for the driver to open the door for her. Annoyed, he took his sweet time rounding the car, and, with attitude, opened the door. "Your chariot awaits," he said sarcastically, waving her into the car.

Lauren rolled her eyes and began to tuck herself into the seat when she noticed Sydney sitting on the opposite side. Her heart skipped a beat, but she played it cool. "What are you doing here? What happened to your car service?"

"Don't talk to me," Sydney snapped. She turned her body toward her window, leaving not much more than her back for Lauren to watch.

Under normal circumstances, Lauren would have tore her a new one. But now she knew why Sydney was trippin'. For the first time, Lauren realized that her twin thought she was complicit in her boyfriend's affair with Dara. And what could she possibly say to that? She did have some intel on Dara having a bit of carnal knowledge of Marcus, and she never once said anything. So she wasn't completely innocent in all of this. But she wished she could tell her sister she didn't know how deep it had been between Marcus and Dara.

And how sorry she was that she'd done nothing to stop it from going that far.

19
SYDNEY

"There has to be a reason," Sydney whispered to herself over and over as she lay motionless on her bed facing the slowly rotating ceiling fan. She had stopped feeling the breeze on the stream of salty tears running down the side of her face hours ago. In fact, she had pretty much stopped feeling anything at all since she ran out of her Aunt Lorraine's house the day before. Sydney flipped over on her stomach and reached for the picture frame on her nightstand. Inside was a photo of the twins when they were just three years old. The two girls sat on either side of their mother unwrapping gifts under the Christmas tree. It was one of the few keepsakes from the years before Keisha married Altimus that she actually allowed the girls to keep out in plain sight.

As she slowly fingered the frame, Sydney examined the

old photo closely. As often as she'd looked at this picture over the years, she'd never really thought about just how many gifts were actually under and around the tree. For a so-called dead-ass-broke family in the hood, there seemed to be way too many gift boxes. Dice's words rang in her ears: "You need to be careful and pay attention." Counting as many as twenty big gift boxes in this photo alone, it didn't take a rocket scientist to figure out that her parents weren't living quite as broke down as Keisha loved to assert. The sound of her bedroom door opening interrupted Sydney's train of thought. She hurriedly put the photo back down on the nightstand and wiped her face with the back of her hand.

"What did I tell you about closing doors in my house?" Mrs. Duke questioned as Sydney silently stared at her.

"Sorry," she finally uttered from between clenched teeth.

"We're meeting your stepfather at Justin's for dinner tonight," Keisha stated as she cut her eyes suspiciously back and forth between Sydney's flush and tear-stained face and the turned-over picture frame. "You coming?"

"No," Sydney stated sourly.

"Excuse you? And who do you think you're talking to in that tone?"

"I meant, no, ma'am," Sydney grudgingly corrected herself.

"Humph, that's what I thought. Well, suit yourself. I guess you can let Edwina know what you feel like eating for dinner. We won't be long," she said as she turned to walk out the door. Mrs. Duke paused with her back facing Sydney. "Dice Jackson ain't never been worth all that crying. He really ain't." And with that, she proceeded to walk out, pushing the door open even wider behind her.

"Ugh, I hate you!" Sydney said vehemently as soon as she was certain that her mother was out of earshot. Frustrated, she hurled one of her pillows across the room.

A short time later, Sydney could hear the sounds of Lauren and Mrs. Duke leaving the house and getting into Keisha's new CLK. The two of them chatted away about Lauren's chances at Homecoming Queen like it was real news. It seemed like even when she was on punishment, Lauren still had something to talk about with Keisha. Her mom and her sister were like two identical peas in the pod — both beyond trifling.

The persistent knot in Sydney's stomach tightened. She hadn't eaten a bite in almost thirty-six hours. *If nothing else, at least I'll lose a couple of pounds from all this freaking stress*, she thought. As Sydney glanced over at the Gala committee binder sitting next to her chemistry book, she stuck out her tongue. The last thing she felt like doing was reviewing the outstanding-ticket-sales numbers or preparing for what was sure to be another impossible chem chapter test. Sighing loudly, she dragged herself up from her bed and stretched her arms above her head to try to relieve some of the tightness in her muscles. Missing out on her weekly spa appointments was definitely taking its toll. As she closed her eyes and slowly tilted her head to the side, Dice's ominous words continued to haunt her: "I made a lot of enemies, apparently even among those people who were the closest to me." Sydney's eyes snapped open. Her father never once named those people who were closest to him. Why?

Sydney's first instinct was to pick up the nearest phone and call her Aunt Lorraine's house. Then she would definitely know who Dice's friends were back in the day. But placing a call on the Duke landline was too risky. Since Sydney was only allowed to make school-related calls, Keisha was monitoring all outgoing numbers on the landline like a hawk. Sydney then considered waiting till the morning to ask Marcus to borrow his car again, but in addition to the chemistry exam making tomorrow's attendance mandatory, Marcus was slightly suspicious of how long she'd been gone the last time she borrowed his car. He kept insinuating that he didn't necessarily believe her story about going home for note cards. At her wit's end, Sydney was ready to throw herself back on the bed like a five-year-old having a temper tantrum when she remembered the old Christmas photo.

While that might be one of the few mementos from their earlier childhood that Mrs. Duke actually allowed her to display in the house, there had to be more stuff in the storage boxes downstairs in the basement. If there was anything to be learned about her family's past, it was somewhere in the boxes. Filled with renewed hope, Sydney quickly slipped on her fuzzy slippers and headed downstairs.

"What would you like for dinner, Ms. Sydney?" Edwina asked as Sydney passed through the kitchen on her way to the door beside the pantry that concealed the basement staircase.

"Oh, I'm not hungry, Edwina," Sydney said, barely pausing to flip the light switch as she headed down the steps.

"Okay. Do you need any help looking for something down there, miss?" Edwina inquired as she wiped down the already immaculate stovetop.

"It's okay, I'm good," Sydney called back up from the foot of the stairs. For years, Altimus had been threatening to clear everything out and renovate the basement into a game and workout room for himself. "Pay attention, pay attention," Sydney mumbled as she looked around the huge and cluttered space. Sydney noticed her old ten-speed with the same flat tire that put it out of commission over seven years ago next to a pair of beat-up roller skates; a pile of board games; lots of old luggage sets; the huge teddy bears that Altimus had won each of the girls at the State Fair so many years ago; and garbage bags full of clothes that were probably Salvation Army bound at some point.

Sydney slowly walked around the perimeter of the basement. She spotted an old bag of kitty litter from the time

Lauren rescued a stray kitten. Li'l Tigger barely lived in the house for forty-eight hours before Keisha caught him inside her closet scratching her full-length llama-hair sweater. She promptly dropped the poor thing off at the nearest no-kill shelter.

Moving along slowly, Sydney passed an old VCR with countless Billy Blank's Tae Bo tapes piled on top. Next to that was a dusty stationary bike and small, green plastic dumbbell weights from Keisha's fanatical healthy-living stage. Sydney smiled slightly as she remembered the horrible faces her mom used to make as she forced herself to drink a raw-egg-and-protein shake every morning.

Finally, a small pile of dusty brown moving boxes behind several old metal lawn chairs and a huge beach umbrella caught Sydney's attention. She immediately picked her way through and pulled the boxes out into the limited free space. From the looks of the layers of dust, half of the boxes had remained completely untouched since the day they moved into this house.

Sydney struggled to open the first box. Using the edge of a stray wire hanger she found on the floor, she was able to tear the masking tape that securely held the edges. When she finally pulled back the flaps, a faded red-and-white bib with a huge red-and-black ladybug embroidered on the corner was the first item to emerge. Sydney fought to hold back the tears as she stroked the edges of the ancient item. Pulling herself together, she continued to dig through to the bottom of the box. There were a whole bunch of baby clothes but no concrete clues. Stashing the bib in the back pocket of her Joe's Jeans, Sydney quickly threw the rest of the stuff back in and closed the lids. "One down and three to go," she grunted, still feeling hopeful as she ripped open the tape on the next box.

The second box was filled with Mrs. Duke's belongings. An old-school pair of Lee jeans with the big brown logo patch on the back sat at the very top of the meticulously folded pile. Sydney snorted at the idea of Keisha's pretentious butt squeezing into the pair of cheesy acid-washed jeans. As she delved deeper, Sydney found more outdated clothes and shoes, including a pair of white Keds with pink laces. Just before she reached the bottom, her hand hit what felt like an old leather-bound journal. After struggling to pull it out from under the weight of the clothes, Sydney anxiously opened it to the middle pages. Lo and behold, staring right back at her was a huge 9 x 11 photo of the twins with Keisha and Dice taken at the local swap meet. "Wow," she breathed softly.

Sydney reached back in the box to make sure that there weren't any more albums in the bottom and closed it back up. Feeling like she may have found what she was looking for, Sydney carefully pushed all the boxes back to the corner and placed everything back in its prior position as best she could. Then she hauled butt outta there.

"You find everything you need, Ms. Sydney?"

Edwina asked as Sydney hurriedly closed the staircase door behind her.

"Mmm-hmm, I'm good, thanks. I'm just gonna go do some studying," she reassured the old lady as she headed back to the safe confines of her room.

Taking the steps two at a time, Sydney's heart pounded painfully by the time she reached her bedroom. She considered hiding out in her walk-in closet but settled on her bathroom — it was the only door in the house the girls were allowed to close without their paranoid mother busting in like a federal agent. Just to be safe, Sydney grabbed her chemistry book and placed it on her bed as a decoy. Then she took a deep breath for courage and headed into the bathroom.

This time Sydney started from the very beginning. There were several pictures of a very pregnant Keisha at her baby shower, surrounded by a lot of women. The only person Sydney recognized was her Aunt Lorraine. She couldn't believe how many people her mother, the ultimate loner, used to be cool with. Next there were pictures of Keisha and Dice with the girls shortly after the delivery. Both of her parents looked exhausted but overjoyed. Even though the photo was taken no more than a few minutes after the delivery, Keisha still managed to rock a huge pair of gold hoops and hot-pink lipstick. Sydney smirked as she imagined her mother demanding time to freshen up before having the photo taken.

Sydney flipped slowly through countless pages of the girls as newborns and toddlers wearing various matching outfits, including those annoying frilly underpants that mothers with too much time on their hands tend to put on their little girls. With each page turn, Sydney longed for the years before they moved into the big house, when her real family was still intact and the twins were still totally inseparable. She took her time and slowly examined each photo, trying desperately to memorize each one.

Sydney was almost three-quarters of the way through when a candid shot of her father and a friend relaxing on the red leather couch, drinking Heinekens, and watching the television caught her attention. *Where do I know this guy from?* she wondered as she pulled the grainy photo from the page to get a better look. Unable to put her finger on the answer, she replaced the photo and kept flipping. She flipped through several more pages filled with candid pictures of Keisha, her grandparents, and a guy who looked so much like Keisha, Sydney just assumed it was her Uncle Laurence. And then there were a bunch of Dice and the familiar-looking stranger. In one, the tall, dark stranger rocked a serious Jheri curl and posed with Dice in front of a pimped-out black Cadillac with gold rims. They were wearing the exact same outfit from head to toe. "I know him," she muttered under her breath as she tried to imagine what the two men might have been about to get into when the photo was taken.

Suddenly, Sydney heard the front door slam. Startled, she jumped up from her perch on the closed toilet and a large professional photo fell out from the back page. "Stop! You play too much, Altimus," Lauren whined dramatically as Sydney listened to the group heading up the stairs. She quickly bent down to retrieve the picture. However, as soon as she turned it over she froze. It was her parents' official wedding photo: Keisha, Dice, and their entire twelve-person bridal party in all their tacky eighties fashion glory. Once again, the tall, dark stranger was standing right next to Dice. But this time, thanks to the clarity of a professional photo, it was perfectly clear: The stranger — and best man — was Altimus.

Sydney's heartbeat roared in her ears. "Oh, my God . . ." she wheezed. She didn't know whether to run, hide, scream, or just faint. *Mom married Dad's best man. Altimus was my father's best friend!*

"Say it, say it," Altimus commanded playfully from down the hall. "Who loves you more than me, Lauren?" Just the sound of his voice made Sydney break out in a cold sweat.

"Ain't nobody love her more than her damn mother," Keisha interjected.

"Whatever, you're both crazy," Lauren quipped.

Sydney involuntarily dry-heaved. As soon as she regained her composure, she shoved the album under the sink behind the countless bottles of shampoo and conditioner and turned on the faucet. *I've got to talk to Lauren. But she'll never believe me. She's got to know. She'll just sell me out again.* Sydney wrestled with her thoughts as she feverishly rinsed her hands over and over. When she finally got herself together, Sydney turned off the water and dried her hand on the fluffy, white, monogrammed hand towel. It was decided: She definitely had to tell Lauren. All she had to do now was figure out how.

20
LAUREN

"We've got to stop meeting like this," Jermaine said as Lauren climbed the stairs at the MARTA West End Station. "Somebody might think we got a thing going on or something."

Despite that she felt like crap, Lauren giggled and threw her arms around Jermaine's neck, leaning in for a short, passionate kiss. "I was under the impression that we do have a thing going on, Mr. Watson." Lauren pulled back to look at Jermaine's face; she loved it when he smiled and made a habit of sticking her Vamp Black–painted pointer fingernail into his dimples. She remembered once while she was lying around in her room thinking about Jermaine that her mother used to do this to her when she was a little girl. Jermaine once mentioned to her that his dimples were definitely one of his "selling points" with the ladies. "But they're mine, now," Lauren said, feigning jealousy with a pronounced pout. "I might as well put them in my pocket and take them with me." He always seemed amused when Lauren said that.

Jermaine pulled back from Lauren's embrace and looked around to see who all was watching them. It was cold outside — the first real chill of the fall season — so there weren't a lot of folks hanging out like usual, just a few stragglers rolling dice outside Nifty's Package Store, which, on most nights, stayed open longer than the clubs. If you couldn't get your drink on at Joy's Gentleman's Club (a strip joint, it was anything but gentlemanly, but nobody ever paid much attention to the name), you could always count on a quick stop at Nifty's to get your after-hours drink on. On this particular night, though, nobody seemed to be paying anyone else who was on the street much of any mind, but Jermaine, still a little shaky from his last almost-run-in with Lauren's daddy, wasn't trying to linger too long out in public. This much Jermaine knew for sure: He didn't want Altimus Duke to know that he was the reason his daughter was still hanging out in the hood.

"Come on, let's get outta here," Jermaine said, pulling his hoodie up onto his head and taking Lauren's hand. "It's cold out here. My moms is over at my auntie's house, checking in on my grandmother, so it's cool if we go back to my place."

"What about your brother — he there?"

"Nah — I don't know where he at, and don't really care," Jermaine snapped.

"Okay then," Lauren said, wrinkling her eyebrows. "Your house it is."

On the short five-minute ride to his place, Lauren emptied out her cache of goings-on, starting with the crazy way Altimus was acting in the car, and how she'd written down on that slip of paper a few fake names instead of the real ones, hoping that it would keep Altimus off his trail. She continued with Marcus telling her that he had a bona fide "thing" with Dara behind Sydney's back, and her suspicions that it was Sydney who circulated the ugly story about her encounter on the Thug Heaven video set. By the time they pulled into Jermaine's tiny, gravel driveway, Lauren was running down the entire list of "don'ts" Altimus and Keisha had laid on her as punishment for visiting the West End. "The crazy thing about it," Lauren said as Jermaine opened her car door and took her hand to help her out, "is that both of them are acting as if nothing is wrong — like they don't have me practically tethered to my sleigh bed. I mean, one minute they're taking away every form of communication I own and treating me like I'm in preschool, and the next minute we're going to dinner. Keisha's all treating me to pedicures, and Altimus is throwing hints about some big surprise he's getting for me. He even offered to take me shopping for my Homecoming dress. I just don't get them," she insisted.

"I'm not so sure you really want to," Jermaine said cryptically as he pushed his key into his front door lock and hit the massive piece of wood with his shoulder. "That's what I wanted to talk to you about."

"See, that's what I love about you, Jermaine," Lauren said breathlessly. She eyeballed the living room and kitchen to make sure they really were alone, and then grabbed Jermaine by the tail of his hoodie and pulled him close to her. "You're the only one who truly understands me, who doesn't judge me for who I am or who my parents are, isn't all impressed with it and stuff," she said, planting a kiss on his lips. "You're not like the other boys I've dated. Nothing like them." She kissed him again.

"Look, did you ever think that there might be a chance that your father isn't who you think he is?" Jermaine asked, pulling away from Lauren and taking her hand. This time she instinctively led the way into his bedroom.

"Whose parents are who we think they are?" Lauren asked, twirling onto Jermaine's bed and kicking off her chocolate Chanel ballet flats. "I swear, they spend so much time trying to keep us from doing all the things they know good and well they did when they were our age that they forget we have the right to live our lives the way we see fit. Shoot, I know Keisha was some wildfire back in her day, especially if it's true that you mellow with age, 'cause mellow, she ain't."

She pulled Jermaine onto the bed next to her and drew him close.

"Yeah, you're right about that," Jermaine said, rubbing his brow. "But do you really know any of Altimus's background — where he's from?"

"Of course I do, Jermaine — I mean, he raised me from when I was in kindergarten. He grew up in the hood in Atlanta, father wasn't around, got rich selling cars, blah, blah, blah. I mean, what more is there to know?"

"A lot," Jermaine murmured under his breath.

"Look, there's no reason to be afraid of Altimus Duke," Lauren assured. "He's just an overprotective daddy who didn't take too kindly to seeing his daughter hanging out in a pool hall in the West End. We live in Buckhead for a reason, trust."

"There may have been more to it than that," Jermaine insisted.

"What? Altimus is afraid I might fall in love with someone with less than sterling credentials? Someone who doesn't live in a fancy house or drive one of his luxury rides, or have the phat bank account or go to the right schools or churches? Well, so what? He grew up the same way, and look how he turned out. Besides, Altimus is my father, but he's not Lauren," she said. "Lauren decides who Lauren is with, and I choose you, Jermaine Watson. I choose you."

"There's more to it than that," Jermaine said, shaking his head. "Your father . . ."

"Not in my mind," Lauren insisted. "Not at all. I know who my father is, and no amount of bougie, overprotective bull from him is going to keep me away from you, Jermaine. You're truly the only person who I have ever trusted this much. And you don't let me get away with shit, either. And I'm good with that — for real. All those other boys, they ain't got nothing on you, for real."

Jermaine was quiet as Lauren stroked his face and then ran her fingers down his neck and his arm. He smirked when she gave his biceps, which were pushing against his hoodie, a squeeze. She leaned into his neck and inhaled deeply; she loved the way he smelled — like baby powder, no doubt from the deodorant he'd just applied. Once, when his scent rubbed off onto her sweater (from an extra-long, extra-close hug,) she slept with it in her bed for nearly four days, sending it with Edwina to the cleaners only after she could smell him no more.

Jermaine turned his face to Lauren's and looked into her eyes. He licked his thick brownish-pink lips, then leaned in and kissed her softly. Lauren returned his kiss with a passionate one of her own; they rocked back and forth, holding each other so close and tight that they felt like one.

Lauren pulled back from his lips and his embrace and sat up. She looked down at her hands and fidgeted just a little, trying to find just the right words to say at this precise moment. Jermaine sat up, too.

"What's wrong?" he asked.

"Nothing's wrong," she said. "Really, everything is exactly right." Lauren was quiet for another moment. "Look, after that e-mail was sent out about me being a ho, you asked me why I cared about the people at my school thinking I'm fast. Well, I care because — despite a reputation to the contrary — I'm not fast."

"I know that, Lauren . . ."

"Wait, let me finish, or else I may chicken out and not say what I have to say," Lauren said, raising her finger in the air to silence him. "People at my school think that because I flirt with guys and dress the way I do and don't care about the things my sister cares about that I'm, uh, sleeping around. But the truth is, Jermaine . . ."

"What," he urged.

"The truth is, I've never, um, been with a guy before. Not, um, in the way that people think I have."

"Hold up: You're a virgin?"

"Is that so hard to believe?" Lauren snapped, giving her head a little twist for emphasis.

"No, no, I mean, no . . ." Jermaine said, trying to redeem himself. "I mean, it's just that, you know . . ."

"I know, I know, I'm not shy about rolling up on guys,

right?" Lauren asked, letting out a nervous giggle. "I'm just confident, is all. I know what I want, and I'm not afraid to say it or get it when I want it, and I guess people confuse that."

Jermaine was quiet.

"And if you haven't noticed, I'm picky. And the right guy just hasn't ever come along. All the little boys I've dealt with thought they knew me, which means they thought I'd hook up with them just because. Such a turnoff. The only other person on this earth who knows I've never been with anybody is my sister, which makes perfect sense why she put that e-mail on the blog saying I slept my way through the Thug Heaven set. She knew that would be the one thing that would really hurt me."

"Damn, I don't know what to say, L," Jermaine said.

Lauren leaned in and kissed Jermaine. "Don't say anything," she said as she unzipped her sweater. She looked into his eyes: "I already told you, I choose you, Jermaine Watson. And I want you to be my first."

Lauren peeled off her sweater, revealing a black-and-beige-print La Perla bra, a Christmas present from Keisha. Jermaine stared at her breasts and then at Lauren's eyes. Common sense told him this wasn't a good idea. His body was saying something totally different, and that side won out when Lauren touched his chest and kissed him again.

"Hold up," he said. "Let me just go and get some protection. My brother should have some in his room. I'll be right back," he said, rushing to his door.

When he flung it open, he ran smack into Rodney.

"Hey there, little brother. What's the haps? Little late for company, ain't it?" Rodney asked, leaning over Jermaine's shoulder to look at Lauren, who was hastily pulling her sweater back on. She was mortified.

"Yo, dude, what you doin'?" Jermaine sneered, squaring his shoulders.

"The question is, little brother, what *you* doin'?" Rodney said, his eyes still on Lauren.

"Minding my business, that's what," Jermaine said. "You would be wise to do the same."

"Oh, baby brother, you know any Duke business is my business," Rodney said, smiling.

"How do you know my name?" Lauren asked, pulling her sweater tightly around her chest. The menacing look on Rodney's face made her nervous, as did his hulking frame, which was wrapped in what appeared to be dirty work clothes. The lint in his natty braids didn't help his cause, either.

"Lauren, right?" Rodney said, pushing past Jermaine and into his room. Lauren was silent. "I know your daddy."

"How do you know Altimus?" she asked.

"No, baby girl — not Altimus. Your *daddy* — Dice Jackson."

Lauren did everything within her power not to shudder at the sound of Dice's name falling off Rodney's lips. "He's not my father."

"Oh, he may not be your father, but he's your biological, correct? At least that's what he told me."

"No, I don't know what you're saying," Lauren said, confused. "How do you know Dice?"

"Let me break it down for you, then . . ." Rodney started.

"How about you just go on in your room and leave me to my company, Rodney," Jermaine interjected. Steam was practically rising from the top of his head; his eyes were fire-red.

"Nah, li'l bro — I think your little girlfriend needs to know a few things about Daddy Dearest," Rodney continued. "Daddy Duke and Daddy Dice go back — way back. And Daddy Dice ain't none too pleased that ol' Altimus done prospered so well, especially since he did it on Dice's back."

"Yo, I could kill you right now," Jermaine seethed through his teeth.

"But you won't, li'l bro. Blood can't take out blood — it's against the code," Rodney smirked. "So I'm gonna pretend you didn't say that. That's one for ya."

"Look," Lauren said, standing up and grabbing her coat. "I don't know what you're talking about or what you think you know about my family, but I've heard enough. I want to go home. Now. Jermaine, please," Lauren practically begged. She was scared beyond words and wished she were anywhere but standing in front of this lunatic in the middle of the night in the damn hood.

"Come on, Lauren, I'll get you home," Jermaine said.

"Yeah, run along, young'un. And tell Altimus he might wanna get ready to settle up." Rodney laughed as Lauren and Jermaine broke into a trot past him. "Yeah, tell him it's time to settle up."

Lauren didn't take a breath until she was sitting in the front seat of Jermaine's car, and then she thought she was going to hyperventilate.

"Lauren," he said as he started the car. "Baby, come on — talk to me."

"I. Have. No. Words," she said curtly. "Just take me home."

Jermaine knew not to say anything else. He simply pulled out of his driveway and onto Hopewell Street.

It was 1:24 A.M.

And when they passed him, neither Lauren nor Jermaine noticed Altimus slumped down in the front seat of his car. Watching.

21
SYDNEY

"And by a landslide victory, your new Ms. Brookhaven Homecoming Queen is . . ." Principal Trumbull paused for emphasis. As she stood directly behind him on the podium in clear sight of the entire student body, it was all Sydney could do not to roll her eyes at the overzealous principal's unnecessary dramatics. "Lauren Duke!" he finally shouted enthusiastically into the microphone. Blue and white balloons and silver confetti dropped from the ceiling as the entire ballroom applauded wildly. Sydney took a deep breath and reminded herself to look excited as she clapped along with the crowd.

Lauren, on the other hand, clearly had her look of "genuine" surprise down cold. She batted her eyes furiously and continuously mouthed the phrase "Oh, my God, I can't believe this" as she stepped forward on the stage to accept her crown. Although it pained Sydney to admit it, her sister looked amazing. Dressed in a fitted silver-beaded Dolce & Gabbana gown and Jimmy Choo Swarovski crystal stilettos with a big ol' Beyoncé-esque weave to boot, Lauren was nothing short of ethereal.

Principal Trumbull stepped to one side of the microphone and allowed Sydney to move forward with the enormous crown to the other. When Lauren finally reached the center of the stage, she stopped and turned to look expectantly at Sydney. "Congratulations, sis," Sydney offered diplomatically as she placed the crown on Lauren's perfectly coifed head. Sydney barely pulled her hands away from the crown before Lauren was on the microphone thanking the world like she had just won an Academy Award.

"Thank you all so much, this is such a surprise," she droned on while Sydney scanned the countless faces in the crowd. The Homecoming Benefit Gala traditionally brought out the entire Brookhaven student body as well as recent alumni, and this year was no exception. To Sydney's credit there wasn't an empty seat in the room. For the first time ever, the Homecoming committee had managed to completely sell out all the tickets.

As Lauren finally wrapped up her long-winded speech and headed down to the dance floor for the traditional first dance with the football team co-captain and Homecoming King, Andre Brown, Principal Trumbull leaned over to whisper in Sydney's ear, "I do believe this is the most impressive Benefit Gala in Brookhaven's history."

"Why, thank you, Principal Trumbull," Sydney replied modestly. "I do what I can."

"Keep these fund-raising efforts up, and Brookhaven will have a new library wing before your class graduates next year," he said with an appreciative smile.

Sydney smiled in return as the slow song ended and DJ Quickfingers jumped on the microphone. "All right, y'all, I need everybody to report to the dance floor. 'Cause it's . . . about . . . to . . . go . . . down!" With that said, the first notes of Yung Joc's club banger, "It's Going Down," exploded from the speakers and a stampede of students in formal gowns and tuxedoes rushed to get their swerve on.

"Well, you and that impressive young man of yours be sure to enjoy yourselves tonight," Principal Trumbull offered as he patted Sydney on the back and turned to speak to Vice Principal Lang.

"Will do," Sydney murmured as she watched the two men walk away. Pausing to admire her handiwork before heading back down into the crowd, Sydney had to admit that she was pleased. The past couple of weeks had been no less than a hot mess. It was good to see something turn out right. Now if only she could figure out how to wrap everything else in her life up as nicely, she'd be all right.

"You coming down to join the party or you plan to stand

there looking like the cat that ate the canary?" teased a familiar voice from below.

Sydney looked down from the stage into Marcus's grinning face. Wearing a black tux with white satin tie that perfectly complemented her black-and-white-striped Monique Lhuillier gown, it was easy for everyone to see why the two were considered Brookhaven's best-looking couple. "I'm coming, I'm coming." She laughed at being caught basking in her own glory as she walked above him toward the steps at the edge of the stage.

"Nice job," Marcus complimented as he held out his hand to help her descent.

"Thanks. I believe the word Principal Trumbull used was . . . impressive. Yes, I do believe that's what he said," she said with a sly smile.

"Well, don't get beside yourself now, Syd," Marcus chided gently. "We both know this is just small change compared to how much I helped my mom raise for her campaign last election. I'm proud of your work, but — "

"Whatever, Marcus," Sydney cut him short with an impatient sigh. This was her night and she wasn't about to listen to him sing his own praises. "Do you wanna dance or something?" Sydney asked as she looked toward the crowded dance floor. She easily spotted Rhea in her crimson empire-waist Betsey Johnson dress, finger-snapping it out to Lil Jon's latest remix. Rhea's date, Tim Collins, was a varsity baseball player who sat next to her in Art History class. Although Sydney didn't know that much about him, he seemed more than happy to be wrapping his hands around her best friend's tiny waist.

Marcus looked at Sydney as if she'd suddenly grown a second head. "Are you serious?" he asked contemptuously. "You know I don't do crunk music."

"Me neither," Sydney conceded, wishing he would loosen up sometimes, "but I was kinda in the mood to dance."

"Tell you what," Marcus said as he steered her toward the now empty table where they ate dinner earlier. "I'll go grab us a couple of glasses of punch. By the time we finish with those, the DJ might actually put on some decent R&B music that we can dance to, okay?"

"Okay, fine." Sydney playfully pouted as Marcus pulled out the chair for her to sit in. "Just promise you won't get caught up in a conversation and forget about me!"

"How could I forget about my girl?" Marcus threw back as he headed off to the refreshment table on the opposite side of the room.

Sydney smiled as she watched Marcus cross the floor. As much as she hated to admit it, the boy had swagger. Recently, he'd been on a mission to make things between them right again. And she was falling for it, hook, line, and sinker. She glanced back at the dance floor and noticed Carmen rocking a gorgeous emerald-colored, backless Ungaro gown that she'd seen in a recent issue of *W* magazine. More interesting, Carmen was all hugged up with what had to be the cute boy from the golf-pro shop. Sydney shook her head and smiled wryly. If nothing else, Carmen always had good taste in clothes.

"Um, excuse me, miss. Is this seat taken?" Once again caught daydreaming, this time Sydney looked up into Jason's inviting smile as he indicated the empty chair to her right.

"Hey, you," Sydney responded softly as she took in his sexy charcoal-gray tux and silver bow-tie ensemble.

"I saw that you were by yourself, so I thought I'd come over and say hi. May I sit?" he repeated his request. Sydney instinctively looked across the room toward Marcus. "If it's a problem . . ." he hesitated as he followed her glance.

"Actually," Sydney replied as she watched Marcus on the other side of the room doing exactly what she'd just finished asking him not to do — holding court with his boys from Student Government — "it's not a problem at all." Much to Sydney's annoyance, from the look of his relaxed stance, Marcus's conversation wasn't about to end anytime soon.

"Okay, good," Jason replied as he sat down. "'Cause I didn't want the night to pass without me getting a chance to tell you how beautiful you look."

"Why, thank you, Jason." Sydney gracefully accepted the compliment. "You look really nice, too."

"Yeah, I like to think I clean up okay," he joked as Sydney rolled her eyes playfully.

"Oh, is that so? And I wonder what your date likes to think," Sydney questioned playfully as she made a point of looking around Jason for his missing date.

"Aww, man, I rolled with my boys tonight," he replied easily as he picked up Sydney's hand and admired the huge David Yurman ring she'd "borrowed" from Keisha's jewelry box for the occasion. "Unfortunately, the girl I wanted to ask was already taken." At a loss for words, Sydney looked away from Jason's face and down at her hand, which he still held. "Anyway," Jason cleared his throat and pushed his chair back, "sounds like they're playing my song. You wanna dance?"

"Yeah, sure," Sydney replied. She snuck another glance at Marcus, who was still deep in conversation.

"Cool," Jason said as he stepped back to allow Sydney to lead them out to the floor.

Sydney took lots of deep breaths as she slowly walked in front of Jason. It felt like every eye in the room was on her as she led the way into the crowd. She searched for Rhea and Carmen, but for some reason, she couldn't find either of them. Halfway to the middle of the floor, Sydney stopped and turned to tell Jason that she'd reconsidered. Dancing with the cute football co-captain had just as much, if not more, drama potential as a Friday night run to South City Kitchen, and more drama was the last thing she needed now. But when she saw the gorgeous smile on his face, she immediately changed her mind. "This good enough for you?"

"Works for me," he answered lightly, putting his hand on her waist to get them moving in sync. When he let go, the spot on Sydney's waist tingled lightly.

"Look who joined the party," Carmen called out as she deftly moved through the crowd with her date in tow.

"You better work," shouted Rhea as she pumped her hands to the sounds of Jim Jones's classic, "Ballin'," on her way over to join the crew.

Sydney smiled gratefully at her friends. Both Carmen and Rhea knew the unspoken good-girlfriend rule: Even if Sydney was dancing/kicking it with another guy, as long as her girls were around, she always had a built-in alibi. "My friends are hilarious," she giggled in relief as she started to relax and enjoy the moment.

Two songs later, Sydney turned to the beat and caught both Lauren and Dara staring at her, mouths agape. Sydney stepped closer to Jason and put an extra twist in her hips just for their benefit. *Guess y'all aren't the only ones with moves*, she thought as Jason nodded appreciatively at the extra-credit action he was receiving.

"I thought you didn't listen to crunk music," he whispered good-naturedly in Sydney's ear.

"I don't," Sydney teased, "but that doesn't mean a girl can't feel like shaking her behind sometimes."

"Mmm-hmm, shake on," he agreed as the run of up-tempo songs finally ended with Ciara's "Promise." Sydney and Jason stood facing each other uncomfortably as the surrounding couples immediately moved in closer for the sexy slow jam.

"Well, I guess I better head back . . ." Sydney started.

"Yeah, you wore me out, Ms. Thing," Jason agreed. He placed his hand on the small of her back as the two slowly maneuvered through the maze of writhing bodies.

"Thanks for the dance; I had fun," Sydney said over her shoulder as they pushed through toward the edge of the dance floor.

"My pleasure," he responded.

Before she could think of anything else to say, Sydney made direct eye contact with Marcus, who was now standing at their table with his boys, staring her down like she had just robbed his mother. As she stiffened up, Jason discreetly dropped his hand from her back. "Shit," she hissed under her breath.

"You good? You still want me to walk you over?" Jason asked warily as he spied Marcus and his friends posturing.

"Um, actually I'm good," Sydney said as diplomatically as possible. She could tell from Marcus's face this wasn't going to be anything nice.

"All right then, enjoy the rest of your night, pretty girl," Jason said with a soft squeeze of her arm. Sydney didn't dare turn to watch him walk away.

"You having a good time, Sydney?" Marcus's best friend, Todd, was the first to speak as she neared the group.

"Actually, I am. You?" she tossed back sarcastically as she ignored the tittering of the group of boys.

"What do you think you're doing?" Marcus asked nastily.

"Um, I was just about to sit down," Sydney replied, choosing to ignore the implied meaning of his loaded question.

"Don't be cute, Sydney," Marcus warned menacingly. "You think I'm stupid? I turn my back for two seconds and there you are, playing yourself with some wannabe, half-literate jock." A low chorus of oohs and ahhs echoed from his friends as they began to scatter from the scene like flies.

Sydney's eyes flashed in anger as she slammed her cherry-red clutch down on the table. "Marcus. The only person playing himself is you by acting like a jealous fool behind the quote unquote half-literate jock," Sydney spat back. "Maybe if you spent more time handling your business at home and not chasing down strays then you wouldn't have to worry about me being around Jason!"

"Oh, so you admit that you were with him the other day!"

"Wait, what?" Sydney asked, completely confused.

"You know what I'm talking about! You didn't leave school to go back to your house the other day! Just admit that you used my whip to go see Jason!"

"Go see Jason? Oh, Marcus, please! Stay focused! You're just mad 'cause you assumed that I'd just wait for you to return to the table no matter how long you took. So when you finally remembered to come back and I wasn't here, you got your little feelings hurt! Two seconds my behind!"

"Whatever, Sydney, that's besides the point."

"Just how is you doing what you want at my expense besides the point? Oh, wait, I forgot. It's all about you. I'm just the lucky one who gets to come along for the ride, huh? Listen, Marcus, don't let your little friends get you gassed. We both know what the deal is," she hinted as she noticed Rhea and Tim walking over from the dance floor.

"I have nothing more to say to you right now," Marcus said, nervously pulling his hair back and trying to make it seem like he wasn't fazed by Sydney's comment.

Sydney paused and looked at Marcus. She considered how relaxed and at ease she felt during those few times she'd hung out with Jason, compared to the constant pins and needles she walked on to be the perfect girlfriend to Marcus. She just didn't want to do it anymore. "I'll do you one better. How about, I don't have anything to say to you ever again. How about that?"

"You all right, Sydney?" Rhea asked upon arrival as she looked suspiciously from her obviously upset best friend to Marcus. "You need to step outside or something?"

"Actually, Rhea," Sydney said, "I think my night may have just come to an end. Would you guys mind giving me a ride home tonight? The carriage I arrived in is officially a pumpkin."

22
LAUREN

"I have to see it again," Keisha announced as she practically bounced into Lauren's room, smiling and giggling like she was the one who won the Homecoming Queen crown. It was the third time that evening alone that Keisha parked herself on Lauren's bedroom chaise to discuss the details of the Ms. Brookhaven Prep Homecoming Ceremony and relive her glory days as the girl who took the crown in her junior year at West End High. Lauren wasn't sure if it was the semiprecious sparkles in the jeweled crown that had Keisha all drunk with her delusions of grandeur, but she did know that she was tired of her mother interrupting her quiet time. As much as she thought she'd be happy about standing dead center in the Homecoming court in her fabulous gown and hearing her name called — and as beautifully as she played it off — Lauren wasn't as giddy as she thought she'd be about being named the flyest chick in her school. Without Jermaine there to congratulate her, dance with her, and hold her, the title and all the trimmings that came with it — the serenade, the traditional Homecoming Queen walk, the crown — felt, well, insignificant. Well, just a little. She had a good time dancing with Andre, and an even better time watching the sparks fly when Sydney cut Marcus's doggish ass off. Tonight, though, Lauren just wanted to finish watching the last ten minutes of *Law & Order SVU*, catch the first ten minutes of the news, then go to sleep so she could wake up, get to school, and IM Jermaine about her weekend. Couldn't none of that happen with Keisha buzzing in and out of her room.

"It's over there in the box, in the same place it was the last time you came to visit it," Lauren said, pointing lazily at the heap of mess on top of her bureau.

"Don't act like you're not excited by all of this, sweetie," Keisha clucked as she peered into the box. "This crown right here says you're the baddest girl in your school, which means that all the money, time, and effort I put into turning you into a Mini-me paid off."

Lauren rolled her eyes and tried her best to concentrate on the argument the defense lawyer on *Law & Order* was making for why the teenage boy on trial wasn't the real murderer.

"I still don't understand why you only have one picture to show me," Keisha continued, oblivious. "Didn't anybody have a digital camera? I figured someone would have e-mailed you some pictures by now. Dara doesn't have any?"

Lauren wasn't about to go into details with Keisha about why she and Dara weren't speaking — the blog about her Thug Heaven debacle, her knowing about Marcus's affair with Dara, the whole Sydney brouhaha on the dance floor — all of that needed to be kept from her mother's knowledge bank lest she take the Homecoming Queen sash and strangle Lauren with it. It was bad enough she was sitting up in her room at nine-fifty on a Sunday night, hair wrapped, pajamas on, with absolutely no means of communication to speak of to get to her man; the last thing she needed to do was set Keisha off and get into it with Sydney again. "Dara's spending the next few days with her dad and didn't have time to download her pictures yet," Lauren said easily. "I'll check tomorrow to see if the yearbook committee has any more they can forward."

Keisha, still lost in her own thoughts, fingered the one printout Lauren did have on hand, given to her by the staff photographer who snapped all the Homecoming shots. "Well, you certainly look beautiful in this one," Keisha said. "Not as fly as I was when I won, of course, but you look good. Too bad I don't have any pictures of that day to show you — had this bad dress on and a flyboy on my arm. Girl? Who you tellin'? You don't know nothin' 'bout that!" Keisha said.

"It was a nice moment, Mom, it really was. I wish my man

was there to see it. Um, Donald, that is," Lauren said, trying to clean up her major slip. "I really wanted him to be there. I mean, Andre Brown is handsome and all, and looked good in his Homecoming crown, but he wasn't the one I wanted to go with."

"Oh, stop it with the Donald mess," Keisha snapped, tossing the picture back onto Lauren's bureau. "I know you're not still holding on to the whole 'Donald is my boyfriend' charade."

"Mom, I don't care what Sydney told you, I did not — nor do I think — that Donald is gay. He's a little, well, *extra* sometimes, but gay? I couldn't have missed that," Lauren insisted. Of course, admitting she knew would have opened her up to more questioning and exposed the pack of lies she'd told her parents over the past two years about who she was really with all those times she was supposed to be out with Donald. Nope, Lauren wasn't falling into that trap, either.

"Yeah, well, if his own daddy thinks he's gay, he just might be. A parent knows, Lauren," Keisha warned. "A real parent knows."

"Wait, wait," Lauren said, turning back to the television screen. "This is the part I've been waiting for — they're about to break down this witness and find out his big sister had something to do with the little girl's murder."

"Oookay," Keisha said. "That's my cue. I'm outta here. Congratulations, again, sweetie. You're now a part of a rare group of girls who can forever claim Queen Bee status around these parts. I knew you had it in you, baby," she added as she leaned down and kissed Lauren.

"Thanks, Mom," Lauren said weakly, forcing herself not to roll her eyes.

Her mother walked out just as the *Law & Order* credits started rolling; Lauren missed the whole ending. Normally, she would have used the digital-video-recorder device on her cable box to rewind the show so she could see what she missed, but Lauren needed to flip over to *Fox News at 10*, a show she watched regularly for at least ten minutes every night to see what the weather would be like the next morning so she could plan her wardrobe and hairstyle accordingly. Annoyed, she settled back into her pillow and yawned while the news anchor droned on about the beluga whales at the Georgia Aquarium, the baby panda at Zoo Atlanta, a robbery at a Quick Trip in Marietta, and a hit-and-run in Gwinnett County.

"This just in: Fulton County police are investigating the brutal murder of a man found bludgeoned to death on his own front lawn. Police say Rodney Watson is a recently paroled convict who spent almost six years in prison for running a small drug smuggling operation out of his mother's West End home."

Lauren bolted up in her bed and stared at the screen, trying to process just what in the world the anchor was talking about. Had she heard him correctly? Did he say Rodney Watson? As in Jermaine's brother? Lauren grabbed her remote and pushed the rewind button to hear the reporter's words again.

"Watson was found about an hour ago on his front lawn, where police say his body lay for two hours before an anonymous witness called police. Tonight, police say they're looking at two persons of interest, including Watson's own brother, and a recently paroled former convict who lives in the neighborhood. We'll have more on this investigation as it continues."

Lauren pushed pause and jumped out of bed, tears welling in her eyes. What in the hell was going on? Jermaine's brother was dead? And her man was being sought in his murder? Lauren didn't know what to do with herself. She paced furiously from one side of her room to the other, stepping on shoes and clothes and papers she'd carelessly dropped there earlier when she settled into her TV-watching position. She raced over to the cordless house phone buried beneath her laundry and dialed Jermaine's home number and then cell phone, unconcerned at that particular moment about the repercussions of using the land line to call some guy in the West End. She needed to find out if he was all right. But both phones just rang and rang until they finally went to voice mail. Lauren pushed "end" on the phone and paced back and forth in front of the television, looking at the still image of Jermaine being led away in handcuffs. The tears that had puddled in her eyes ran hot streaks down her face. And before she could get ahold of herself, she was running toward Sydney's room.

"Get the hell out of my room," Sydney practically spit as Lauren burst through the door without so much as a knock.

Lauren paid her sister no mind. "Come to my room — you have to see this," she whispered.

"What are you talking about? I'm not coming to your room to watch any damn TV — some of us have better things to do," Sydney said, slamming her pen down on her notebook for emphasis.

"Sydney, please, just listen to me," Lauren implored, moving close enough to her sister for her to see her tear-streaked face and red eyes. "Something's popping off with my boyfriend, and . . ."

"Boyfriend?" Sydney sneered. "What happened, he got stuck in a boy sandwich down at his dream all-boy school?"

"I'm not talking about Donald," Lauren said. "I'm talking about my boyfriend, Jermaine."

"Jermaine? Who is —"

Lauren cut Sydney off. "Please, Sydney, come into my room. It was just on the news. Just come with me."

Sydney sucked her teeth, slowly rose to her feet, and reluctantly followed Lauren into her bedroom, but the frantic, frightened look on Lauren's face made her stomach curl.

"Look," Lauren implored as she hit rewind and then play on her cable box's digital video remote.

"Ohmigod, Rodney is your boyfriend?" Sydney asked, obviously still confused.

"No — no! Jermaine is my boyfriend; Rodney is Jermaine's brother."

"What happened?"

"I don't know," Lauren sobbed. "I was just watching the same thing as you just did and I called Jermaine and he didn't pick up and I don't know what to do because they think he killed his own brother."

"Wait, Lauren, calm down," Sydney said. Finally, she recognized the gravity of the situation. "They said he's a person of interest — not the person who did it."

"What's a person of interest?" Lauren asked.

"I don't know," Sydney said. "I don't know, Lauren. I just don't understand all of this. How do you know those guys?"

Lauren sat down on her chaise and buried her face in her hands. "It's a really long story," Lauren said.

"Tell me," Sydney said, walking over and sitting next to her sister.

Lauren sighed and recalled for her twin how she met Jermaine, how they'd been kicking it over the past month, and how her love affair with the man who'd thoroughly turned her out came to a crashing halt the day Altimus walked into The Playground and found her cursing out Jermaine's hood-rat ex.

"Wait, Altimus saw you in the West End?"

"Yeah," Lauren said, reaching for a tissue.

"What was he doing there?" Sydney inquired.

"I don't know — business, I guess," Lauren said, confused.

"Was he there with somebody? Did he have paperwork spread out? Was he selling somebody a car?"

"I don't know, Syd. God — what you do you want me to say?"

"Think!" Sydney yelled. "I need to know why Altimus was in the West End."

"Why? He's not the one in a police station somewhere getting beat down and forced to cop to something he didn't do — Jermaine is!"

"Look," Sydney snapped, "I can tell you this right now: I think Altimus has something to do with this."

"Altimus? Why Altimus, Syd? He's our father, and he's always loved us and treated us like his own daughters," Lauren insisted, though she was trying just as much to convince herself of this as she was Sydney. She got a chill just conjuring up a mental image of Altimus leaning into her face in his car that day on the side of the highway, after he'd busted her in the West End. And then just as easily as Lauren defended her stepfather, she remembered what Rodney said to her the last time she saw Jermaine. She put her hands to her mouth, wishing that her hand could reach back and erase the words Rodney spewed. "Ohmigod," she yelled.

"What!" Sydney said. "What is it?"

"Oh, no, no, NO!" Lauren said, a fresh round of tears working their way up from her gut.

"Lauren, come on, tell me," Sydney said, grabbing her sister's wrists and looking her in her eyes. "What do you remember?"

"The last time I saw Jermaine, Rodney walked in on us and said he knew Dice."

"Dice? How does he know our father? Go on," Sydney urged.

"He didn't say — just that he knows him. And then Jermaine threatened Rodney. He told him he could kill ·him. Oh, God, what did he do? *What did he do?*" Lauren broke down.

"Shh," Sydney said, rubbing Lauren's back to try to comfort her. "Listen, I wouldn't be so quick to ask what Jermaine did."

"Then Dice — what about him? I know he's capable of something like this," Lauren sneered. "Maybe he thought Rodney would do something to you or me to get at Altimus. That's possible, right?"

"Dice is not capable of beating a man to death," Sydney huffed, pulling back from Lauren.

"Sydney, look, I know you love him and all, but Dice is a criminal through and through. Even if he got busted for running guns, how do you know he didn't pick up a few new bad habits in the Big House? Tell me that! I mean they said on the news that the other person of interest is a recently released former convict. That's Dice!"

"Because I know our father. He wouldn't do something like this."

"But I know Altimus, and he wouldn't do anything like this, either."

"Don't be so sure," Sydney said. She got up and disappeared into her room, only to emerge with a timeworn photo in her hands. She thrust it into Lauren's face.

Lauren looked at the picture and squinted a little. "This is Mommy and Dice's wedding photo?"

"Yes."

Lauren ran her fingers over the picture. "What does this have to do with anything, Syd?"

"Look closer," Sydney said. "Look at the wedding party."

Lauren leaned into the photo a little more. "That's Altimus standing next to Dice, isn't it?" she asked her sister.

"Yes."

245

"They . . . they knew each other?" Lauren gasped.

"Yeah," Sydney said, embracing her sister.

Lauren leaned her head on Sydney's shoulder. And right then, at that moment, she knew that the only person on this earth that she could trust and hold on to was Sydney.

23
SYDNEY

"Um, so tell me again how many times you were on that thing by yourself," Sydney asked incredulously as the girls drove past the MARTA West End Station and headed up Lee Street toward Ralph David Abernathy Boulevard.

"Oh I don't know, five or six," Lauren said simply as the Saab's navigation system shouted out directions. "Honestly, Syd, it got to the point where I wasn't even nervous about it anymore. It was just a means to an end. Isn't that crazy?"

"What's really crazy is that Mom and Altimus actually believe that bogus Homecoming Court bonding-retreat excuse you gave them this morning," Sydney answered with a wry smile. "I swore they'd never let either of us touch a car key again. And, voila, not only do you have your car, but we don't even have a curfew for the day."

"Hey, let's just say I've had a little bit more practice than you when it comes to lying," Lauren retorted. "Besides, Keisha's so geeked about me winning Homecoming Queen she'd probably buy me a ticket to the moon if I told her it was one of my duties. I mean, she and Altimus have been talking about a big surprise for us and everything because of it."

"Touché, touché."

"But all jokes aside, sometimes I think I would go to the end of the earth to be with Jermaine. Wait till you meet him. He's really . . ." Lauren started to choke up.

"I believe you, sis," Sydney gently put her hand on Lauren's shoulder to calm her. The last thing she wanted was Lauren to have a breakdown and crash the car. There's no way in the world they could explain away the car being towed out of a ditch on this side of town. "Please don't get upset, everything is going to work out. You see they had to let him go. Trust, if there was any evidence contrary to his innocence, there was no way the Atlanta police would've released him from custody."

"You're right," Lauren sniffled as she pulled herself together. "It's just a lot. I'll be okay as soon as I actually see him with my own eyes."

"I feel you." Sydney's voice trailed off as she thought about how badly she wanted to see Dice. She would have never guessed in a million years that Lauren was right when she suggested Dice may have had something to do with

Rodney's murder, but sure enough, they'd arrested her dad in the whole mess. Unlike Jermaine, the cops had used her father's parole as a reason to detain him indefinitely. Sydney used Rhea's phone to call Aunt Lorraine's, but nobody answered. She just continued to pray for the best as she followed the story in the *Atlanta Journal-Constitution*.

"There it is," Lauren broke the silence by pointing down the road to the Antioch Baptist Church sign at the end of the long driveway leading up to a medium-size building and a very full parking lot.

When Lauren originally told Sydney that she decided to skip school and sneak over to Jermaine's brother's funeral service, she thought Lauren had finally lost what little common sense she had. Not only did they not have access to a car, but Lauren hadn't been in touch with Jermaine at all since the arrest. But she was determined, and there was simply no way Sydney was about to let her sister go by herself. However, now that they were facing a church full of folks who might know about their dad, or worse, Altimus, Sydney started to have some serious second thoughts. "You sure about this, Lauren?" she asked as they neared the driveway.

"No," Lauren answered honestly as they pulled into one of the last available parking spots in the lot. "But I'm sure that I need to see Jermaine. I need to know that he doesn't blame me."

"Okay, then," Sydney said as she inhaled deeply and

unbuckled her seat belt, "let's do this." With one last check in the vanity mirror, she was out of the Saab. Trailing slightly behind her sister toward the entrance, Sydney surveyed the full lot. Everything from a beat-up Toyota Camry to several pimped-out Benzes filled the parking spaces. It seemed like half the hood had come out to pay their respects to Jermaine's brother.

Lauren stopped when she reached the entrance. The sound of the organ could be heard clearly through the heavy mahogany doors. "I didn't see his car out here. If we wait in the foyer, hopefully we can catch him before he walks in. What do you think?"

"That's fine," Sydney said as she tugged nervously at the pearl earring in her right earlobe. She was only eleven when Nana Jones, her mom's mom, had passed. Since then, she hadn't had much experience with funerals. Lauren straightened her posture and took a deep breath before opening the doors. Sydney made a quick sign of the cross and followed right behind.

"Welcome to Antioch Baptist, ladies. The services have yet to begin. Please feel free to walk in and have a seat," directed the usher as he handed them both funeral programs.

"Actually, we're waiting for someone else," Lauren responded.

"Okay, that's fine. But please step to the side while you

wait," he answered, pointing to an area out of the way of incoming traffic.

"Thanks," Sydney said as she stepped to the side and admired the poster-size portrait of Rodney posed in front of what she assumed was his pickup truck.

"There's a lot of people up in here, Syd," Lauren whispered in Sydney's ear.

"Mmm-hmm," Sydney agreed as she peeked into the sanctuary. Seemed like almost every pew was filled except for the first two. Rodney's shiny black casket lay closed directly in front of the pulpit. She wondered if that was the family's choice or because the body looked a mess.

"I still can't believe this is happening. This whole situation is just so crazy," Lauren said as she started to work herself up again.

"It's okay, Lauren, it's okay," Sydney said, trying to soothe her sister with a hug. "We'll figure it out. Don't worry, we'll figure it all out." She just hoped that her words sounded much more convincing than she actually felt.

"Oh, no, they didn't," hissed a very angry-looking young woman with a baby as she entered the church. "I can't believe the both of them had the nerve to show their faces!"

"Guess they think all that money gonna make this right," her companion, a short light-skinned girl with braids and bad acne, added. Lauren and Sydney took a precautionary step back as both women sucked their teeth viciously and proceeded into the sanctuary.

"Was that the girl you cursed out at the bar?" Sydney asked, turning to face her sister.

"No," Lauren said, sounding just as surprised as Sydney. "I think I kinda recognize the girl with the baby from that day, but I never spoke to her or her fat friend."

"Well, sounds like she knew you, or I guess I should say us," Sydney said nervously. "Hey, wait a minute. You never confirmed what Rodney said about Dice being your father, did you?"

"No, never."

"Oh, okay. Then I wonder why she sounded like we were to blame."

"Listen, I have no idea what the hell she was talking about," Lauren said as she ran her fingers through her hair nervously, "but I ain't come down here to get my ass kicked. That's for damn sure!"

Sydney nodded her head in agreement as she watched more mourners enter the church. It seemed that every time someone looked over at Rodney's portrait and noticed the twins, there was a flurry of whispers and dirty looks thrown at the girls. Sydney moved protectively in front of her sister when she thought she overheard a group of young men say, "We oughta send Tiki to slap that ho up."

The volume of the organ music suddenly increased. Sydney looked at Lauren, who shrugged her shoulders in return. The usher walked over to the girls. "The service is about to begin. You should take your seats."

"Is it gonna start without the family of the deceased?" Lauren snapped.

"Lauren!" Sydney instinctively reprimanded. "Um, I'm sorry about that — she's just a little emotional," she offered, hoping to diffuse the situation.

"I see . . ." the usher said as he pursed his lips with much attitude.

"We're actually waiting for the brother of the young man; I mean, Rodney. So if it's okay, we'd prefer to remain out here," Sydney continued with her best fake smile.

"Well in that case, I guess you may remain." The usher turned on his heel and walked away.

Lauren sucked her teeth at his retreating back. "Whatever . . ."

"Forget it," Sydney said as she touched Lauren's shoulder lightly. "That's not what we're here for."

"Speaking of what we're here for, here comes Jermaine," Lauren said as she looked over Sydney's shoulder. Sydney turned and watched one of the cutest boys she'd seen in a minute enter the church holding the elbow of a forty-something-year-old woman who bore a striking resemblance to Rodney. As the usher addressed the woman, who Sydney assumed was his mother, Jermaine's eyes connected with Lauren.

"Lauren, you're here!" he exclaimed, as he immediately stepped away from the woman and headed over to the twins.

"How could I not be? I was so worried about you," Lauren answered as he swept her up in a tight hug. The two clung to each other for a minute before Sydney finally cleared her throat. "I'm sorry. Sydney, this is Jermaine. Jermaine, this is my sister, Sydney," Lauren said, finally introducing the two.

"Wow," Jermaine said as he tried to hide the surprise in his face. "It's nice to finally meet you."

"I'm really sorry for your loss," Sydney said sincerely. When she considered all the horrible things that Lauren had probably told him about her before today, Sydney was glad he was able to even slightly contain his surprise.

"Um, yeah, thanks," he said sadly.

"Jermaine, you coming?" the woman demanded in a shrill voice.

"Yes ma'am," he replied respectfully. "Y'all should sit with us up front," he offered. "I don't think there's going to be that many empty seats left."

"Okay," Lauren said, taking his hand confidently.

"Good idea," Sydney said simultaneously, as she thought about all the shade they'd received earlier.

Jermaine led the girls back over to the entrance. "Mom, I'd like you to meet my girlfriend, Lauren," he said, indicating Lauren.

"Humph," she huffed, clearly uninterested in meeting anyone.

"It's a pleasure to meet you," Lauren said. "I'm so sorry about Rodney."

"And this is her twin sister, Sydney," Jermaine pointed at Sydney.

"I'm so sorry for your loss ma'am," Sydney said.

"'Preciate it," Jermaine's mother said as she fanned herself with the program. "Well, I guess the usher will jus' have to walk me in since you got your little girlfriend here and whatnot."

"Um, there really ain't no seats left. Is it okay if they sit with us up front?" Jermaine asked quietly.

"Do what you like, Jermaine; I'm here for Rodney today."

The usher stepped forward and asked, "Are you ready, Sister Watson?"

"If one is ever ready to bury her own child," she replied, taking his hand as the tears started to roll. "Lord Jesus, give me the strength. I need it now. I need it now." The doors opened and Eugenia Watson slowly headed into the sanctuary; Lauren shot a quick look at Sydney.

"You guys ready?" Jermaine asked as he inhaled deeply.

"Don't worry about us, we're good," Lauren answered as she gave his hand a quick squeeze. "As long as I'm with you, it's all good."

"Okay, then," Jermaine responded gratefully as he led the two inside.

As they walked down the aisle to their seats, Sydney watched her sister and Jermaine. She'd never seen Lauren so submissive, ever, let alone to a so-called boyfriend. There was definitely something different about her when she was with Jermaine.

"Bitch," a skinny brown-skinned guy with a black T-shirt suddenly hissed at Sydney as she passed. Sydney gasped in surprise but managed to keep her eyes straight ahead and avoid eye contact.

As soon as they were seated, the services began. The pastor delivered a moving eulogy that caused many of the women to shriek out loud and even fall out of their seats. "Why, why, why?" screamed a voice from the back above the cries of a baby. Sydney cringed from all of the obvious emotional pain in the air. More than anything, she prayed.

"Dear God, please do not let Altimus be responsible for any of this," she mumbled to herself when the congregation was asked to bow their heads. "And please, please, please, keep Dice safe."

Before long the service ended and the sanctuary started to slowly clear out. Jermaine's mother remained in her seat, rocking back and forth. "Lord, please take care of my child. Please, Lord, I beg of you," she whispered in a grief-stricken voice.

"Mom," Jermaine said as he softly touched her shoulder.

"Just leave me, 'Maine," she said. "I need a few more minutes with my baby."

"You sure?" he hesitated.

"Go on, boy, I'll see you outside," she instructed sharply.

"Yes, ma'am." He recoiled slightly. Sydney could see the hurt zigzag across his face as Jermaine straightened up and indicated to Lauren and Sydney that he was ready to leave. The three walked out in silence. Sydney braced for the crowd they were sure to meet when they stepped outside.

"Yo, Jermaine, what's up with shorty showing her face here?" asked a tall, dark-skinned guy dressed in a white T-shirt with Rodney's image on the front.

"Yeah, man, why either of them hookers here? Is you disrespecting your dead brother like that?" a short, fat bald guy with the same T-shirt said as a small crowd started to form around Jermaine and the girls as soon as they hit the sidewalk.

"Relax, Tone," Jermaine responded. "I asked her to be here." Sydney and Lauren looked at each other nervously as the crowd grew more agitated.

"Naw, bump that. You know who their father is. You know what he did to your blood. That's jus wrong, cuz," insisted the same dark-skinned guy who called the twins out when they were standing by Rodney's portrait before the service.

"Yeah, you need to hold them tricks hostage and send that fool Altimus a message," insisted another guy who Lauren thought she recognized as Don from the night at the bar. "Coming round here acting like they don't know what's up when bitches straight live with a killer."

"Babe . . ." Lauren whispered worriedly to Jermaine. Sydney started measuring the distance to the car in case she needed to break out in a run.

"Yo, like I said. Be easy. They're with me," Jermaine said again, this time his voice much more threatening. "Ain't nobody disrespecting my guests or my brother's memory except y'all." He turned to Lauren and asked, "Where'd you park?"

Sydney pointed in the direction of the Saab. "Over there," she answered in a very low voice.

"Let's go," Jermaine said, stepping forward confidently. To Sydney's relief, the crowd parted to let them pass.

"Don't let me catch either of you tramps alone after dark," called out a high-pitched female voice as they passed.

The group walked toward the car in complete silence. Jermaine never once let go of Lauren's hand. When they finally arrived, Lauren searched her bag for the car keys.

"So, what? Is everyone just going to act like that didn't happen?" Sydney questioned, unable to remain quiet a moment longer.

Jermaine sighed and rubbed his head. "I don't want to bring you guys into this mess," he said reluctantly.

"Well not for nothing, seems like we're already in the middle of it, no?" Lauren stated more than asked as she finally pulled her keys out and clicked the alarm.

"Fine, but remember, you asked," he said as he looked down at his shiny black shoes. "So basically, your stepfather ain't really a car dealer. On the real, he been running things in the hood Godfather-style for years."

"Ohmigod," Lauren squeaked.

"I knew it. I knew it. Please go on," Sydney encouraged him to continue.

"Rodney was on the same block in prison as Dice. That's why your father is a suspect, because they knew each other and, well, as you know, Dice has got a pretty shady past. Supposedly, Dice put Rodney on to a lot of the shit that Altimus was doing. Which is why everyone in the hood thinks that Altimus had reason to have my brother killed. But you should know that Rodney was a lot of things, but he wasn't no rat," Jermaine insisted.

"But . . . but how could you know this about my family and still want to be with me? How come you didn't say anything until now?" Lauren asked incredulously as she searched his eyes for clues.

"Once I spent time with you, I knew in my heart that you had no idea about Altimus. And I guess I just figured that when you were ready to talk about it, you'd tell me about Dice. As far as I was concerned, none of what Rodney was talking about was hard, cold facts, and it didn't have anything to do with me personally . . . until now. But let's just say what I know for sure is that I didn't kill my own brother. And whoever did, well . . . he's gonna pay."

24
LAUREN

The limousine driver pulled into the circular driveway of the Duke estate at precisely 5:30 P.M. Lauren and Sydney, who had spent the afternoon primping and posturing in front of the mirror — with warnings from Keisha every fifteen minutes to have their behinds downstairs in time for their ride — had been sitting in the parlor since 5:00 P.M., watching Altimus run through the house in his tuxedo, fetching everything but the kitchen sink for his bossy wife, who was upstairs in her expansive walk-in dressing room, being plucked, prodded, combed, and tucked to perfection. She had a team of three men up there giggling and gossiping with her — one to style her hair, one to paint her face flawlessly, and a third to make sure that every inch of her body looked absolutely perfect in her exquisite black, knee-length, Christian Lacroix Couture party dress. By 5:35 P.M., it was clear that regardless of how much she had harassed everyone else to be on time for the big anniversary event, Keisha wasn't about to rush her grand entrance for anybody. They could wait.

"I wish this night was over already," Lauren huffed. "I'm so over it."

"I'm with you there," Sydney said, crossing her legs. Then she whispered: "Honestly, I can't believe we're about to party it up, particularly with what all is going on with Rodney and Jermaine and Daddy. I'm finding it extremely difficult to concentrate on all of this."

Lauren nodded. "I mean, look at Altimus, running around here like nothing — like he doesn't have a clue what's going on!" she said, a little too loudly for Sydney's comfort.

"Shh," Sydney warned. "We don't know if Altimus had anything to do with this. We can't be sure who did that to Rodney. Anyway, just because the police say they have suspects doesn't mean the people they arrested actually did the crime. Marcus's mom is always talking about how important it is that we question . . ." She got quiet. Over the past few days, Sydney had tried hard to put the whole Marcus mess behind her — thinking of the greater good that was going to come from being single. *But how,* she kept asking herself, *do you just cut off your feelings for someone after a four-year relationship?* She'd figured out a lot of things about herself and

Marcus over the past few months. But the answer to that question? Not so much.

Lauren looked at her sister and then down at her hands. "Thinking about Marcus, huh?" she asked quietly.

"I ain't studying him," Sydney snapped. "He deserves neither my time nor attention. Forget him."

Lauren knew her twin better than that, though. She chose her words carefully: "Look, Syd, I know you're mad at him and how all of the stuff with him and Dara went down. I was a total bitch about it. I should have told you what was going on, but I need you to know that I didn't know how far the thing with him and Dara had gone. All I knew is that he and Dara kissed once, but both of them swore to me that it was a mistake and it wasn't a big deal. You and Marcus —"

"Are through," Sydney said, cutting Lauren off. "I don't care if it was just a kiss, he shouldn't have done it."

"And I should have known what was going on, for real, and let you know. I'm sorry about that, sis," Lauren said.

"You were definitely wrong for that," Sydney said, looking into Lauren's eyes. "I guess I just thought he and I would be together always. It's funny how blind you become when that's all that's on your mind. I should have seen it. And I'm not so sure I would have taken kindly to your news if you did tell me about it, so don't sweat it. It's over.

"Besides, that's the least of our worries right about now," she continued.

"Tell me about it. Our stepdad may be the murdering black Al Pacino up in this piece," Lauren said, shaking her head.

Just as Sydney was about to respond, Keisha called down from the top of the stairs. Both girls jumped, startled by her voice and the sight of Altimus curled around her arm. "Come on, tell your mother how hot she looks," Keisha said as Altimus led her down the long, winding staircase.

"You look great," Sydney practically mumbled, as Lauren threw a cheerleader fist in the air and whispered, "Hoorah."

"She does look stunning," Altimus said, watching his wife walk toward the foyer. "Now I know why we've been together all this time — she knows how to keep a brother interested. Hmm, hmm, hmm," he added.

Sydney looked at her watch. "Well, we should be heading out, huh? The driver's been here for about forty-five minutes."

"Honey, he's getting paid enough money to sit his behind in that car for another two hours and not be the least bit mad about it, so don't worry about him. Come on now, get your coats and let's go," Keisha said, clapping her hands to hurry the twins along. "Honey, did you call the photographer to let him know we're on our way? I want him to snap us getting out of the limo when we get to The Sun Dial."

"It's all done, dear, don't worry. Let's just get moving — I'm hungry."

Altimus ushered his three ladies into the limousine and then climbed in himself before the driver shut the door. The limo had hardly started moving before he reached for the bottles in the bar. The limousine company had been instructed to have all the ingredients Altimus needed for his signature drink — the Rusty Nail — and they made good on it, stocking the bar with extra-large bottles of Glenlivet and Drambuie for Altimus's drinking pleasure. Keisha was too busy looking in her mirror and fiddling with the music to pay him much mind, but the girls both watched him, both of them wondering if their stepfather did, indeed, have blood on his hands.

"We've been through a lot, haven't we, Keisha," Altimus said after his first round settled into his stomach.

"Yes, baby, we sure have," she said, patting his knee. "Most of it good, huh?"

"Yes, yes," he said, taking a sip from his second drink. Lauren wondered how many he could put away before their fifteen-minute trip to The Sun Dial came to an end. She looked at Sydney, who, by then, was staring out of the window and fiddling with her earlobe. Altimus kept talking. "I'd say ninety-nine percent of it has been good, you know? That's because we know what family means, and honor and respect the bonds that hold it together. You guys are blessed — you know that, right? We all are."

"That's right, baby." Keisha smiled.

"We're blessed because we love each other, and protect one another, and stick together, no matter what," Altimus continued slowly before taking another sip.

"You better tell it," Keisha said.

Lauren and Sydney exchanged glances and wondered if Altimus's sauce sermon was a cryptic confession. They both came to the same conclusion: He was creeping them out. And Keisha? Oblivous.

"I have a surprise for you," Altimus said suddenly.

"For *moi*?" Keisha giggled, leaning in to kiss Altimus on the cheek. "I'm so excited!"

"Oh, I got plenty for you later," Altimus said, turning to kiss Keisha full on the lips. Both girls grimaced. "I meant I have a surprise for our daughters," Altimus clarified.

Sydney seemed unimpressed, but Lauren, ever giddy over presents no matter what the situation, had to restrain herself from clapping. "A surprise?" she said, after which Sydney elbowed her in the side. "What?" she said.

"Stop acting like you've never gotten anything before," Sydney chastised, giving her the eye for good measure.

"Oh, you're going to love it, Pumpkins," Altimus continued. "The question is, should I give you the surprise now, or should I wait until after the festivities?"

"I'm sorry, but you'll be quite busy after the festivities," Keisha cooed.

"True," Altimus said as he reached into his tuxedo breast pocket. He pulled out a Tiffany box and handed it to Lauren, knowing that the sight of the trademark blue would make his daughter lose her mind.

"There's only one box?" Lauren asked as she tore into the ribbon on the box and flipped the top open. Inside were two horseshoe-shaped pieces of silver. "Um, it's uh, cute," Lauren said, holding one up between her fingers. "What is it?"

"Yes, there is only one box — I didn't want to mess up my lines with two," Altimus laughed. "They're key rings."

"Lovely," Sydney said, uninspired, barely reaching for the ring that Lauren was dangling in her face.

"How, um, nice — a key ring," Lauren said, unable to hide her disappointment over not getting the set of stackable gold rings she'd been eyeing for no less than four months. She wasn't about to buy them herself; she firmly believed that jewelry was meant to be received, not purchased.

"Oh, but why don't you ask me why I'm giving you both key rings," Altimus urged.

"Why?" Lauren insisted, getting back a little bit of her excitement.

"Should I tell 'em babe?" Altimus asked Keisha.

"Oh, go on ahead and tell them, already," she said. "We're almost at The Sun Dial."

"Okay, okay," Altimus said as he reached into his pants

267

pocket. "I got you key rings because you'll need them for these," he said, producing two identical shiny keys in his hand.

Both Sydney and Lauren frowned. What the . . .

"These are the keys to your new condo," Altimus said simply. He settled back in his seat and let the hysteria commence.

"Our new condo? We have a condo?" Sydney screeched, grabbing onto Lauren as she snatched the keys out of Altimus's hands. "Our own place?"

"Well, it's in both of your names, so it is officially your place," he said, smiling.

"Don't get it confused, girls, you won't be living in the condo tomorrow, throwing wild parties and acting like you don't have any parents to speak of," Keisha warned. "We're hiring a management firm to lease it for the next year or so until you two are ready to go off to college, and then when you're about to graduate, we'll upgrade your new place and then you can move in."

"Ohmigod," Lauren shouted. "Yes!"

Sydney was a little bit more reserved, but not much. "Thank you, Altimus, this is one heck of a surprise! I can't believe you bought us our own place; this is incredible."

"Don't sweat it," Altimus said as the limo pulled up in front of the restaurant. "Anything for my daughters. This is about keeping the wealth in the family. You all can live in it, or rent it out for income while you go to college, and then have a place for yourselves when you get your degrees and come back to Atlanta to help your old man with the business."

Lauren and Sydney looked at each other, their twin intuition letting them know that they were thinking the same thing: Since when were they Altimus's recruits for running the dealership business? And who said they'd be living in Atlanta forever?

Keisha checked her makeup in her handheld mirror one more time and told her girls to do the same. When they were ready, the driver rushed around to the back of the limo and opened the door for them. As Lauren stepped out of the long black car, a photographer clicked away. It felt, she thought, like the red carpet treatment; she couldn't help but grin as tourists and fellow Atlantans alike stopped and stared at the power family as it strutted into the building and was escorted into one of the glass elevators, which whisked the Dukes more than 700 feet above the city and opened into a wonderland of red roses and sparkling candlelight. As the photographer continued to snap pictures, the entire restaurant broke out into applause, with many of the guests — a veritable who's who of Atlanta's black elite — hoisting their elegant glasses of champagne into the air in Keisha and Altimus's honor.

Sydney clapped politely as Lauren waved and struck her poses, soaking in the attention and, no doubt, making sure her light was right in every frame of the photographer's film. After an ovation worthy of a Prince concert, Keisha finally waved the photographer away, and, within seconds, the elder Dukes were swallowed into a crowd of congratulatory hugs and well-wishes.

Sydney peered around the room and took in the faces; for just a moment, her eyes searched for Marcus and his mother. And then, deflated, all of it came rushing back to her: There was no more Marcus. For the first time since, like, forever, Sydney Duke was making a very public appearance without her finest accessory on her arm. Well, without being Marcus's accessory. She was keenly aware of that difference.

Lauren caught a glimpse of her sister and hung her head. She fingered the horseshoe key ring in her hand and looked at her twin. Their eyes locked. "Let's go sit down," Lauren mouthed as she grabbed two glasses of ice water from the bar.

It didn't take long for the girls to spot their table — Keisha made sure of that. Sprays of fine roses dripped from the sparkling table, which was decked out with a mountain of candles, crystal champagne flutes, several bottles of fine champagne and wine icing in two gold wine chillers, and special gold-rimmed place settings Keisha made the staff at The Sun Dial purchase exclusively for her party. The sight of it made Sydney just shake her head, continue past the extravagantly decorated table, and head toward the window. Lauren followed.

"Look, Syd, it's going to be okay," Lauren said, rubbing her sister's back as the two of them stared down over the breathtaking 360-degree view of Atlanta. Lauren had always loved coming to The Sun Dial; as touristy as the restaurant had become, it was still quite an exhilarating feeling to stand next to the window as the tower slowly circled the panorama of the city's skyline, watching as Atlanta passed by. When she was a little younger, Lauren would call out the names of all the landmarks she could recognize, always starting with Centennial Olympic Park and the CNN Center, and working her way over to The World of Coca Cola, the Georgia Dome, and Turner Field, and always ending with Stone Mountain, which seemed like it was so far away, it couldn't possibly be a part of Georgia — the Dukes' Georgia.

"How is it going to be okay, Lauren?" Sydney asked as she ran her fingers over the window. "The last few days have been absolutely surreal. I don't know if I'm coming or going anymore, if I even am who I thought I was — if any of this is what we ever thought it was. How do we make sense of all of this?"

"You got me on that one," Lauren whispered. "One minute we're thinking Altimus is an overprotective killer, the next he's buying us luxury condos and stuff. I mean, what can we do? How do we figure out the truth?"

Just then, Lauren stopped looking at the Atlanta skyline and focused instead on the reflection in the glass, which revealed a dark figure approaching them. Sydney grabbed Lauren's hand to signal her to stop talking; both flinched when Altimus wrapped his arms around the sisters.

"The prettiest girls in the room," he said, squeezing the two. "I have to be the luckiest father in the world."

"And you know this," Lauren said, shaking her weave.

"I love you two as if my blood runs through your veins, you know that, right?" Altimus asked. "That's why I work so hard. That's what real fathers do. They set up a future for their families and their families' families, so that everyone can eat and be comfortable and enjoy life. I do what I do because you are my hearts. And I need you both to know that I'm going to always take care of you and your mother, by any means necessary," he added quietly.

Sydney and Lauren looked at each other's eyes in the reflection.

And Hotlanta swirled at their feet.

Acknowledgments

DENENE

For God, who keeps opening windows for me when it seems all doors are closed — without His grace, I am surely nothing. For my husband and darling daughters, Mari and Lila, and my son, Mazi: It is for you that I do what I do — thank you for your constant encouragement, support, and love, which makes each of my words tumble easily to the page, even the stubborn ones. With you all and Teddy by my side, all things are possible. For my parents, Bettye and James Millner, and my brother, Troy Millner: Thank you for loving me hard and strong — you all helped mold me into the woman I am today. For Angelou, James, Miles, Cole, and my in-laws, Migozo and Chikuyu: Thank you for helping Nick and I find our way and providing us with the family structure and friendship that has surely added 20 years onto each of our lives. For my fabulous niece, Imani, and all her sister-friends: Thank you for the Georgia Peach prototypes; your insight into The A helped us find what we think are authentic ATL voices. For Victoria Sanders, my agent extraordinaire: Thank you for keeping me working and constantly challenged — you truly are my Dreamgirl! For our fabulous editor, Abby: Thank you for the deft touch, the deep understanding of all things cool as hell, and especially the laughter — it truly was a joy to work with you. For Andrea Davis Pinkney: You have been a constant source of inspiration for this writer — a mentor when you didn't even know it. Thank you for showing me the way.

And for Mitzi, who keeps me young, fresh, and fly: You are a true star who deserves her own spotlight and theme song, fo sho. Thanks for being my partner.

And finally, thank you to the great state of Georgia, for welcoming my family with open arms and helping us find peace . . . there's no place like home.

MITZI

As always, I begin by dedicating this book to God, Yemaya, all the orisha and guides who have helped me safely arrive at this point in life. Every day offers a new opportunity. Thank you for continuing to open the doors.

Mommie, achieving greatness often requires large leaps of faith. Thank you for always being there on the other side.

Melissa, being your older sister is the hardest job I've ever wanted. Thank you for your patience.

Daddy, the most powerful statements are often unspoken. In case I don't say it enough, I love you.

Roy, loyalty is a priceless trait. You are the bestest cousin ever!

Mommy Sally, words can't express how grateful I am to you and your loving family for accepting me as one of the fold.

To the rest of my relatives — thank you for your love and support.

Joan, you are the fabulous big sister/mentor I've been searching for all these years. I'm so glad I got you in the divorce.

Rhea, sometimes it takes a lifetime to get to know certain people. And then there are others with whom it seems you've already shared a lifetime. I'm so glad you're my girl.

Mali, Carmen, Shayla, Toya, Lisa, Daina, Kenya H., Carla, Dara, Karina, Geoff, Betina, Nicole W., Jen K., and all the rest of my fabulous friends: thanks for the love, support, and inspiration.

Denene, it is such a pleasure working with such a dynamic writer. Thanks for staying focused, making me laugh out loud, and always keeping it moving.

Andrea, Abby, and the entire Scholastic team, thank you for making my *Hotlanta* dreams a reality. From start to finish you guys have been nothing short of phenomenal.

Victoria, thank you for your continual professionalism throughout the project.

Drama, you may not be able to read (or bark), but I know you understand every single word I say. Just think, every day we're a little closer to a big backyard just for you!

And a special shout out to Satonja, my ride or die homie since FAMU. Thank you so much for answering all my late-night pleas for direction (literally). You are truly one of the great ones!

The editors would also like to thank the following for their contribution to the cover image:

Photography: Symon Chow
Model: Danielle Austin
Hair: Stephano, Edris Salon
Makeup: Romy Parscale
Fashion styling: Dorcia Kelly
Jewelry by Annie Basulto for Cubannie Links

To Do List: Read all the Point books!

By Aimee Friedman

- [ ] South Beach
- [ ] French Kiss
- [ ] Hollywood Hills
- [ ] The Year My Sister Got Lucky

- [ ] Oh Baby!
  By Randi Reisfeld and H.B. Gilmour

- [ ] Hotlanta
  By Denene Millner and Mitzi Miller

By Hailey Abbott

- [ ] Summer Boys
- [ ] Next Summer: A Summer Boys Novel
- [ ] After Summer: A Summer Boys Novel
- [ ] Last Summer: A Summer Boys Novel

By Claudia Gabel

- [ ] In or Out
- [ ] Loves Me, Loves Me Not: An In or Out Novel
- [ ] Sweet and Vicious: An In or Out Novel

By Nina Malkin

- [ ] 6X: The Uncensored Confessions
- [ ] 6X: Loud, Fast, & Out of Control
- [ ] Orange Is the New Pink

By Jeanine Le Ny

- [ ] Once Upon a Prom: Date
- [ ] Once Upon a Prom: Dress
- [ ] Once Upon a Prom: Dream

PNTCHK3

Point

www.thisispoint.com